THE HUSBAND'S SECRET

DEBRA WEBB

INTRIGUE

Recycling programs for this product may not exist in your area.

ISBN-13: 978-1-335-69067-8

The Husband's Secret

This is a work of fiction. Names, characters, places and incidents are either the product of the author's imagination or are used fictitiously. Any resemblance to actual persons, living or dead, businesses, companies, events or locales is entirely coincidental.

For questions and comments about the quality of this book, please contact us at CustomerService@Harlequin.com.

Harlequin Enterprises ULC
22 Adelaide St. West, 41st Floor
Toronto, Ontario M5H 4E3, Canada
www.Harlequin.com

HarperCollins Publishers
Macken House, 39/40 Mayor Street Upper,
Dublin 1, D01 C9W8, Ireland
www.HarperCollins.com

Printed in Lithuania

"The only thing I need is for you to understand who I am and why I'm here." Ben smiled hopefully. "And maybe to trust me."

Brenda appeared to consider all he said before she spoke again. "So, I'm supposed to believe that you're here to protect me." She shook her head, her expression weary. "I'm sorry, Ben, you seem like a nice guy, but I need something more concrete than your word. This is my daughter's life—my life—we're talking about here."

"Fair enough." Ben reached for his cell phone and put through a call. "Victoria, I'm here with Brenda Devers. We need to have that face-to-face."

"Give me one minute," Victoria said. "I'll set up a video call."

"She'll call right back, using video," he explained. "Meanwhile, feel free to search the Colby Agency on the web. You'll find images of Victoria and Jamie. They run the agency. You'll see the reviews. Read them. Then you'll understand."

Whether Brenda realized it or not, she could not be in better hands.

Reader Note

I am having such fun creating new stories for the Colby Agency. Please know that I have the utmost confidence in law enforcement at all levels. Anything depicted in this story that might suggest otherwise is strictly fiction and for the purpose of creating tension. Also, please know that when I choose a setting or a particular street, it sometimes requires that I add an alley behind a row of houses, for example, or take away an element that might actually exist in the setting. So, please enjoy the story and watch for the next one coming soon!

Debra Webb is the award-winning, *USA TODAY* bestselling author of more than one hundred novels, including those in reader-favorite series Faces of Evil, the Colby Agency and Shades of Death. With more than four million books sold in numerous languages and countries, Debra has a love of storytelling that goes back to her childhood on a farm in Alabama. Visit Debra at debrawebb.com.

Books by Debra Webb

Harlequin Intrigue

Colby Agency: The Next Generation

A Colby Christmas Rescue
Alibi for Murder
Memory of Murder
Witness to Murder
The Husband's Secret

Lookout Mountain Mysteries

Disappearance in Dread Hollow
Murder at Sunset Rock
A Place to Hide
Whispering Winds Widows
Peril in Piney Woods

A Winchester, Tennessee Thriller

In Self Defense
The Dark Woods
The Stranger Next Door
The Safest Lies
Witness Protection Widow
Before He Vanished
The Bone Room

Visit the Author Profile page at Harlequin.com.

CAST OF CHARACTERS

Brenda Devers—She buried her husband a month ago... but then she sees him at the airport in Los Angeles. Is she losing her mind, or has this all been a huge mistake?

Janey Devers—Brenda's four-year-old daughter, who is caught in the middle of a terrifying ordeal. When she's kidnapped, Brenda's world shatters completely.

Scott Devers—The husband. Victim or criminal? Alive or dead? No one seems to know.

Ben Clark—One of the best investigators at the Colby Agency. He's prepared to do whatever necessary to protect Brenda and to find her child.

Detective Warren Shelton—There are times when Brenda is certain the police don't want to find the truth.

FBI Special Agent Jarrod Cummings—It's difficult to tell if he's one of the good guys.

Victoria Colby-Camp and Jamie Colby—Victoria, with the help of her granddaughter Jamie, will ensure the Colby legacy goes on for another generation.

Chapter One

Tuesday, May 5
Los Angeles International Airport
1 World Way
Los Angeles, California, 5:00 a.m. (PST)

Brenda Devers felt exhausted and so ready to get home. She missed her daughter.

Maybe it was the past few weeks catching up with her. She stared out the wall of glass at the planes taxiing past on the tarmac. Realistically she understood that it was a number of things combined. It was the fact that her estranged husband had died just three weeks ago. They hadn't lived together in nearly a year, but he had fought the divorce process for the past six months as if their relationship wasn't over. Worse, he had flatly refused to negotiate custody terms—at all.

She pushed aside the troubling thoughts and decided she needed caffeine. Desperately. It was way too early to be functioning…even on West Coast time.

Rising to her feet, she reached for her wheeled bag. She pulled it along behind her as she wove her way through the crowd in search of the nearest coffee bar. The line was fairly long, but she had time. Her flight wasn't until six fifteen.

This trip had been a whirlwind. She had waited until Sunday afternoon to take a flight from Huntsville, Alabama, to Los Angeles. All day Monday and well into the evening had been spent in meetings. If she had been able to get on a flight last night, she would be home by now. But that wasn't possible. Instead, she had settled for the earliest possible flight this morning, and still it would be midafternoon before she was home.

She missed her little girl. Needed to be there for her child, who was missing her mother as well as her father.

Late last week when Brenda received the request for an appearance at this meeting, she had really wanted to decline. But her agent had insisted that if she wasn't able to attend in person, things might not go as well. She really wanted Brenda to be there.

Frankly, if Brenda hadn't so desperately needed this deal to go the right way, she would have just said no regardless of the results. Who wouldn't understand that her daughter needed her—she'd just lost her father. Granted Janey was only four years old, but she fully comprehended the situation. Her father was dead… He would not be coming back.

Considering his sudden death, Brenda supposed on some level it was a blessing that Scott had moved out of the house they shared all those months ago. She cringed at the thought. Felt guilty, no matter that none of it was her fault. As awful as it was for her to think that way, she had to be realistic here. Obviously their daughter had grown accustomed to only spending every other weekend with him. If there was any sort of upside to this tragedy, the distance created by the separation had to be it. Still, Brenda felt like a terrible person for thinking such a thing.

What kind of person looked at death with an eye toward finding the upside?

Anger stirred deep in her belly. Perhaps one who kept her head in books—specifically the ones she wrote—rather than in real life. How many times had Scott said those words to her? He'd accused her of being too busy with her career to be a good wife.

Their world had been picture-perfect, he had insisted, until *she* decided a separation was in order. But the truth was, the picture-perfect part had stopped being true five years ago when she'd learned of his first affair—at least she hoped it had been the first one. Sure, she was a big girl who could overlook one indiscretion—one mistake—if he was truly sorry. If he genuinely intended to make sure it never happened again. And particularly since she'd found out she was pregnant with their first child around that same time.

And for an entire year things had appeared to be better. Then came another affair and the subsequent apology. But it wasn't until that second one—no, that wasn't right. It was the third one, at the end of his second period of repentance, that she was done.

Brenda rolled her eyes. She had been such a fool. Or maybe just desperate to keep their family together given they had a child. But sometimes a woman just had to admit it was over and move on.

Last year Brenda had reached that place. Perhaps it was his over-the-top and utterly unreasonable reaction to her book being optioned for a movie only weeks after its release that was the final straw. Yes, she had been hurt and angry when she wrote *The Wife's Diary.* After two affairs and two promises that it would never happen again, the third affair was reason enough to be both. Writing the book had been like a balm to her soul. A way to slough off all the pent-up emotions.

It wasn't like she had used his name…though she had

dedicated the book to him. Maybe it had been just a little nasty of her, but she wasn't the one who had cheated multiple times.

Since making their separation legal and filing the necessary papers, she hadn't felt guilty at all…until the explosion. Having him die suddenly in such a horrific way, of course, made her sad. She had been in love with him at one time. Madly in love with him. But he had slowly but surely destroyed that love. She would not live her life with a man who had so little respect for her that he felt having affairs was completely acceptable as long as he apologized.

Finally, it was her turn to order. Brenda bellied up to the counter and suddenly realized she had no idea what she wanted. She'd been in line all this time and should have figured that out by now, but she had been too caught up in all the awful business of her failed marriage.

"Just coffee," she finally blurted, her frustration roaring in her brain. She really, really needed to be home with her daughter.

The barista stared at her, one eyebrow cocked higher than the other. "What size?"

The grumbling behind her had Brenda glancing over her shoulder.

She opened her mouth to answer the question, then froze…stopped breathing entirely.

"Short? Tall? *Grande?*" the barista insisted impatiently.

Brenda walked away from the counter, her gaze glued to the man she had spotted in the crowd.

Her brain refused to analyze what her eyes were telling her.

It was impossible. Of course it was. Her mind…

He was walking away now, only a few yards ahead of her. If she walked faster she would catch up to him and could reach out and… He suddenly paused and glanced toward something or someone across the hospitality area.

Brenda stalled in her tracks.

A woman hurried toward him. Blonde…tall…smiling.

When the blonde reached the man, she kissed him on the cheek.

Brenda's jaw dropped. This couldn't be right. Then the man smiled. Brenda only saw his profile, but she knew that lean jaw…that smile so well…

"Scott?"

She had called out his name before she realized she'd opened her mouth.

The man who could not possibly be her dead husband glanced back at her.

Brenda stood there, one hand on the handle of her wheeled bag, like a deer caught in the headlights of a massive truck barreling toward her.

The man blinked and then looked away, put his arm around the blonde, and they continued forward.

The shock holding Brenda in place suddenly fell away like melting ice slipping from rooftops after a winter blizzard. She rushed after the man and woman.

"Scott!" she called again.

The two didn't slow. In fact, they seemed to be walking faster. Brenda did the same. A crowd of passengers from a deboarding plane abruptly poured from a gate, and Brenda had to weave through the thicker mass of bodies now going in both directions.

By the time she cleared the new throng, the man and the blonde had disappeared.

Brenda stood in the center of the long, wide terminal corridor. Scanning the faces, she turned all the way around.

Where had they gone?

The bank of elevators nearby…the escalators…one of the other gates…the restrooms.

One by one she walked through the waiting areas of each gate. She scrutinized the faces in search of the man who looked exactly like her dead husband and the blonde she had never seen before—but who was exactly his type.

She checked every food service and dining area. Every single shopping spot. From there she went into each of the ladies' rooms and checked the stalls—waiting for the closed ones to open. Then, with a big breath, she entered each of the men's rooms and did the same. For the most part people ignored her. She'd expected someone to rant at her or to call security. Not that she would have blamed them—her behavior was a little disturbing—but she was on a mission.

Ultimately, she had to admit that they were gone. Either the couple had boarded a plane already or exited the terminal.

Brenda wandered back to her gate, her bag trailing behind her. She surely imagined the whole thing. She'd been thinking about Scott and the past and suddenly there he was. As a writer, she'd done enough research in the field of psychology to realize that during times of extreme stress and/or emotional trauma the mind could play tricks on a person. The eyes…the ears…even the heart could be less than reliable during times of anxiety on such a high level.

She lowered into a vacant seat. It was possible the man had only resembled Scott.

But when she'd said his name he'd glanced back, then quickly looked forward once more. In that infinitesimal moment she had seen something in his face. Surprise? Fear? Or maybe some other emotion that wouldn't have been there if he were a stranger? Recognition, perhaps?

Was it possible he looked like her dead husband and also had his name?

Sure. Obviously it could happen. Seemed a stretch, but life could be surreal like that sometimes.

No. Brenda shook her head. She must have imagined it. She'd been deep in worrisome thoughts about her daughter and her husband's affairs. The whole thing was likely some manifestation of her anxiety and frustration. This seemed far more logical. More reasonable.

Really, she needed to stop looking back and start looking forward. This movie thing was really happening. They were months, maybe even years, away, but her novel was being made into a movie. No more hoping the dream would see fruition—it was a sure thing. It was a rare privilege to have reached such an amazing milestone.

Whatever the release date, next year or the year after, it was real. A smile pulled across her lips. Her agent had been right. She'd had to be in LA for yesterday's meetings. And now, she was going home to celebrate with her favorite other human! Janey would be so excited.

No more looking back…only forward.

Chapter Two

Devers Residence
White Street
Huntsville, Alabama, 3:30 p.m. (CST)

"Hello! I'm home." Brenda closed the door behind her and abandoned her wheeled bag. She tossed her handbag onto the sofa.

"Mommy!" Janey rushed from the kitchen. Her beloved nanny, Mallory Lawrence, hung back but gave Brenda a big smile and a wave.

Brenda crouched down and hugged her little girl until she started to wiggle.

"Too tight," she said with a giggle. "Did you bring me something?"

Brenda released her and wrinkled her nose as if the question were ridiculous, then she smiled. "What do you think?"

Janey grinned. "Yes!"

While the child prowled in her mother's suitcase, Brenda pushed to her feet. "Shall we order your favorite pizza for dinner?" Figuring out something to prepare was the furthest thing from her mind just now.

Janey glanced up, nodding enthusiastically. "Cheese!"

"Cheese it is then."

The four-year-old waved the gift shop bag that held an angel necklace and did a little happy dance. Then she dashed off to her bedroom.

"She does love cheese pizza," Mallory said, walking across the room to give Brenda a quick hug.

Brenda had never been more grateful for Mallory than she was the past few weeks. Having the convenience of a childcare giver who could move in at a moment's notice for an extended stay was a true godsend.

Brenda laughed. "Please don't tell me you had it for dinner last night."

Mallory smiled and shook her head. "Lunch today."

"Oh no." Brenda scrubbed at her forehead. "I'm sorry. I should have asked."

Mallory waved her off. "Don't worry about it. I should get going anyway." She smiled. "Peter is taking me out tonight."

Peter was Mallory's boyfriend. They had been dating for two years. Brenda expected a proposal anytime. Selfishly Brenda hoped a wedding wouldn't change their working relationship. Janey loved Mallory. Neither Brenda nor Scott had any living parents, and they were both only children. Sadly, most all the people at Scott's memorial had been his work friends. When had they stopped having real mutual friends?

Sometimes Brenda couldn't help thinking how sad the whole situation had been. The disconnection to family had never been more overwhelming than it was now. With him gone, their daughter had no one except Brenda. And Mallory.

Brenda pushed the worry aside. She'd gone there entirely too often since the accident. Continuing to dwell on the subject was not good for her mental health or for moving forward.

"Well, thank you." Brenda sighed. She had considered telling Mallory about the man she saw in the airport, but she didn't want to sound paranoid. And the whole encounter sounded entirely paranoid.

Mallory gave her another hug. "Any time you need me." She drew back. "I mean it, Brenda. Call me anytime. I know how hard things are right now. I want to help any way I can."

Brenda nodded. "I will. Thank you."

Mallory smiled, her eyes sparkling. "Your book is going to be a movie!"

Brenda laughed. "It is."

They hugged again, and then Mallory was on her way. Brenda stood at the door for a bit after she drove off and watched as the last of the parents picked up their kids from the school across the street. She really loved this neighborhood. The idea that Janey would be able to attend school right here across the street was the reason she'd chosen this house. She had known from the day she got married six years ago that she wanted to live near the school her children would attend.

Since she was a writer, she worked from home. It was the perfect situation.

After a minute or two, Brenda closed the door, wheeled her bag into her bedroom and prepared to clear it out and stash it away. The house was small. An historic bungalow in Huntsville's famed Five Points Historic District. It was a quiet neighborhood, and walking to the supermarket was one of her favorite parts of living here. The downtown entertainment district and historic square were a mere mile to her left, with tree-lined sidewalks the whole distance. Same with the supermarket to her right—less than half a mile, actually. Most anything she might need was either within walking distance or available via delivery.

And there were really good neighbors. She didn't know any of them as well as she might like, but they were always friendly and considerate.

This house was one of the best choices of her adult life. Scott had never been happy here. He had far grander ideas. Ten months ago, after the separation, he'd bought a mansion on the mountain above Jones Valley in an exclusive gated community. There wasn't even a playground. But the move had confirmed for Brenda that it was over. He had known full well she wouldn't move, and he obviously hadn't cared.

She put her suitcase away in the closet and took her toiletries to the little en suite bathroom. The efficient bathroom and larger walk-in closet had once been a bedroom, but the former owner had turned the room into the must-have amenities for a primary bedroom. The house still had two other small bedrooms—one of which she currently used as an office. Brenda had really wanted a second child by now. She had thought about adding one of those popular shed type offices when the time came to free up that third bedroom, but her husband had shut down that plan. One was enough, he'd insisted.

That old anger simmered inside her. So much of their marriage she now regretted, no matter that it was difficult to hold a grudge against a dead man. And certainly she did not regret having sweet Janey.

The memory of the man she had seen in the airport nudged her. She picked up her cell phone and found Detective Warren Shelton's number in her contacts. Maybe she should call and tell him about the encounter.

She bit her lip and considered it might not be such a good idea. The whole thing actually sounded a little outrageous now that she'd had time to really think about it. Scott was dead. He'd died in an explosion at his office along with his partner and another colleague. It had been a Saturday morning so, thankfully, the entire staff was not in the building. The only reason Brenda had known he was at the office that day was because it was his weekend to have Janey and he'd had to beg off picking her up until Saturday afternoon. Brenda never minded him canceling his time with their child, but Janey did. She might only be four, but she expected her father to show up when he said he would.

The police were still investigating the explosion. Initially there had been some suggestion of a potential gas leak. But she'd heard nothing else about the cause so far. She understood that the police couldn't share details while they were investigating, but sometimes it almost felt as if she were a suspect. She shook her head. Of course she was a person of interest. One of the victims was her estranged husband.

Brenda tossed yesterday's clothes and her nightshirt into the laundry basket before checking on Janey. Her little girl had recently discovered the world of Barbie and loved playing with the collection she'd received for her birthday last month. Her favorite was the Barbie with the purple hair. That day was the last really comfortable, actually nice time Brenda had shared with Scott. Just one week before the explosion.

She blinked away the memory. Their daughter looked so much like her father, with her coal-black hair and sky-blue eyes. His eyes were the first thing that had captured Brenda's attention. She, on the other hand, had sandy-brown hair—not quite blond, not entirely brown—and brown eyes. Really dark brown eyes. Her little girl hadn't inherited a single one of her physical characteristics. Maybe she would be tall and slim like her father too. Brenda had always struggled with her weight. At a mere five-three, it only took a few pounds to make a difference. Scott never failed to point out a single extra pound.

Not thinking about him.

Brenda wandered back to the kitchen and considered making a sandwich. She'd been so out of sorts at the airport after seeing that man she'd forgotten about coffee or breakfast. Then, on the plane, she hadn't bothered with anything from the lunch menu. Maybe she would just go ahead and order the pizza she had promised Janey.

She pulled her cell phone from her pocket, and the doorbell rang.

Since she wasn't expecting anyone, it was likely a salesperson. Living in such a walkable neighborhood, it was not uncommon to have solicitors popping by more frequently than perhaps in other areas. She didn't mind most of the time. Scott had hated it. He made it a point to be rude to any stranger who showed up at their door.

Brenda chastised herself for thinking of him again. They'd been separated for nearly a year. It should be easier than this.

She peeked out a window to see who had stepped onto her porch. Detective Shelton. How strange. She'd just thought about calling him. Maybe there was news about the investigation. Three weeks seemed a fair amount of time to wait for news, but she really had no idea how long these things took. She did a good deal of research related to criminal investigations for her novels, but fiction wasn't the same as real life. In fiction, all aspects of the plot had to work into a reasonable timeline. Though she tried to keep the details realistic, some things were far more interesting to the reader if the details weren't so close to the real world. In any event, this wasn't a criminal investigation.

She opened the door and manufactured a smile. "Detective Shelton, I was just thinking of calling you." When he didn't smile back, Brenda went on edge.

"May I come in, Ms. Devers?"

"Of course." She opened the door wider in invitation. Once he was inside, she closed it, automatically turned the lock. Since her front door opened directly into her living room, she gestured to the sofa. "Please, make yourself at home."

The detective had been here many times. He took his usual seat on the far end of the sofa. She chose the well-worn side chair. It was her favorite, with its pink-and-white gingham fabric. Something else Scott had disliked about this home—her shabby-chic style and the way she'd furnished it. How had she ever believed they had anything in common?

"Ms. Devers," the detective began, "you're aware that our investigation into the explosion has been ongoing."

"Yes." She nodded, hoping the whole thing was nearing completion. Not that she'd been overly involved in any aspect of what the police were doing, but it was just something else hanging over her head. Along with the insurance business and a million other little things she would love to get cleared up.

"As you know, we initially tried identifying the three victims of the explosion using dental records."

"Yes, you explained this to me." It occurred to her then that she should check to see that Janey was still playing in her room. "One moment, Detective." She hurried into the little hall and peeked into her daughter's room. Her little voice as she spoke for one of the dolls made Brenda smile. She returned to the living room. "Sorry. I just wanted to see that Janey was occupied."

He nodded. "Of course. Anyway, since we weren't able to locate the dentist Mr. Devers used in Nevada before moving to Alabama and the one you listed here in Huntsville had no record of him, we needed another way to confirm his identity. We had much the same issue with his partner."

"Tate Jenner," she said. Like Scott, Tate had no recent dental records. His wife insisted the man had perfect teeth and never saw a dentist while growing up and didn't bother as an adult. Scott, on the other hand, deemed himself too busy to bother—at least he had since Brenda knew him.

"Yes. Since we needed to do DNA for an official identification of the partners, we decided to do it for the third victim as well. We didn't have any way of officially identifying him and hoped that perhaps his or a relative's DNA would show up in some database."

Initially, the third person present during the explosion was tentatively identified by the third vehicle in the parking lot, but that wouldn't make the cut as an official identification.

"You took samples from Janey and Trek." Though Brenda hadn't been concerned about Janey understanding the process, Lena, Tate's wife, had really worried about Trek, her and Tate's son. He was older and quite possibly understood exactly what was happening.

"The results are in," Shelton said, "and we've confirmed the identity of Mr. Jenner and a second man, Clinton Pratt."

Brenda nodded, but a buzzing had started in her ears. What was he saying?

The better point was what he hadn't said. He hadn't mentioned Scott.

"DNA from the remaining victim was not a match for Scott."

Brenda stared at him, her face pinched in surprise. "What?"

The fact that her mind had instinctively and instantly

snagged on the idea that something like this was coming when Scott's name wasn't mentioned among the results did absolutely nothing to lessen the impact. How was this possible?

"Your husband was not one of the victims in the explosion."

Brenda thought of the man at the airport, and her mouth opened to tell the detective as much, but no words came out. What he was suggesting made no more sense than the idea that she had actually seen her husband at LAX. If Scott was alive, he would have told her…surely. It had been three weeks. He would have come to see Janey. He would have been trying to salvage his business. No. This couldn't be right. There had to be a mistake.

Definitely a mistake. This was impossible…wasn't it?

Chapter Three

5:20 p.m.

Brenda had followed Detective Shelton to the sidewalk. She'd been too stunned to remain sitting down after the news he'd shared. For a good three or four minutes she had stared at the empty street after the detective drove away. In the distance the sun was slowly sinking down to touch the skyline of downtown buildings, but still a couple of hours remained before dark. She stared back at her home. Her daughter was in there playing, totally unaware of the news that would upset her world all over again.

Scott had not died in that explosion at his office. For the hundredth time she asked herself how that was possible. How on earth was she supposed to tell Janey?

Brenda blinked. Good grief, she'd forgotten to order the pizza.

Before she could turn on the sidewalk to walk back to her house, a car pulled to the curb and parked on the street just beyond where she stood. For a moment she braced for whatever insanity might be coming next…then she recognized the vehicle.

The new neighbor. What was his name? Ben…something.

Brenda waved, then gave herself a mental shake. She was

supposed to be going inside. She took a breath and started forward, along the sidewalk leading to her small porch. The houses on this street were very close together. All built a hundred or more years ago. White picket fences and loads of flowers and shrubs. The cozy cottage style was one of the draws to the neighborhood. But even this place didn't feel comforting just now. She felt completely alone, confused… and more than a little scared.

What did this latest turn of events mean? For all his flaws, why would Scott fake his death? Worse, kill two of his colleagues? He had an issue being faithful, but she had never once considered him evil…certainly not capable of murder. But the detective had vaguely insinuated as much.

"Ms. Devers, how are you?"

She paused and turned toward the sound of her neighbor's voice. He had a nice voice. Calm. Deep. But it was his smile that set her at ease whenever she encountered him.

In spite of herself, she smiled back. "Fine, thank you."

But was she fine? No. Far from it.

Not even remotely fine. But she had no desire to go into her personal troubles with this man—a stranger, really. He'd only moved in next door two weeks ago. She hadn't even realized the house was for sale. She had noticed that it was unoccupied for a while, but no For Sale sign had gone up. She had imagined the older man who lived there was away on business…maybe pleasure. Honestly, her life had been so unsteady for the past year she barely noticed anything. Her neighbors likely thought she was a snob.

Again, she shook herself. She couldn't quite seem to stay on track. Pizza. She was supposed to order pizza.

"I just ordered pizza to be delivered," her neighbor announced. "Would you and Janey care to join me? It should be here any moment."

When she hesitated, he tacked on, "I could bring it to you when the order arrives."

Brenda found her voice. "That's very nice of you, but Janey is kind of picky about pizza. She only likes cheese."

A quirk of his lips and his smile was back. "That's my favorite too. I ordered one cheese and one with everything." He shrugged. "You never know when a neighbor might drop by."

Brenda never dropped by on anyone, but she got it. He was attempting to be nice. All her neighbors were nice. No matter that she hadn't found the time or the initiative to socialize with them, they had all found a way to show their support for her and Janey after Scott's death.

Except he wasn't dead.

As exhausted as Brenda felt at the moment, she decided to just say yes. Why not? She could use the extra dash of consideration just now.

"I was just about to order pizza myself so, yes, that would be very nice." She hitched a thumb toward her door. "If it's not too much trouble, maybe you could come to our place. I just got back home from a trip to LA and I'm totally spent."

"No problem. I'll see you in a few minutes then."

She paused on her porch and watched through the vines and shrubs as he walked up onto his own and unlocked the door. Benjamin "Ben" Clark—that was his name. From somewhere in Illinois.

The house had been sold and he'd bought it online. She remembered him mentioning something about that the one time they had spoken across the fence from their respective backyards. Right after he moved in, she thought. If she recalled correctly, he'd moved for work and considered himself very lucky to nab this place and be able to move in without waiting for the owner to move out. An expedited closing date had been crucial. Funny how those details came back to her now that she thought about it.

Some days she wasn't sure where her brain was.

Brenda wandered through her house to her daughter's room, where she was still dressing and undressing her dolls.

Janey looked up and smiled. "Blossom likes her new necklace."

She had the angel necklace draped around and around the purple-haired doll she had named Blossom. "I'm glad," Brenda said. "The pizza will be here soon. Mr. Clark from next door is bringing it over."

Janey scrunched up her face. "Mallory says our new neighbor is very handsome but strange."

Brenda couldn't help herself; she laughed. Then she cringed. "Please don't say anything like that to him when he brings the pizza."

Big blue eyes staring up at her mommy, Janey nodded. "Mallory says he kept waking her up when she spent the night. You know when you was at that place about the movie."

"How did he wake her up?" Brenda went on alert. Mallory hadn't said a word about any issues.

"She said he kept coming and going." The four-year-old made a knowing face. "She's a light sleeper, you know."

Brenda bit the inside of her jaw to prevent the new laugh tickling her throat from popping out. "I'll ask her about it."

Janey turned to her other dolls and started talking for Blossom, inviting them for a tea party by the pool. Her new Barbie Dreamhouse had a pool.

Brenda walked back into the living room and checked out the front window. No sign of a pizza delivery vehicle. She might have time to call Tate Jenner's wife. The idea of what the detective had told her still rocked Brenda to the core. It was insane, really.

She pulled her phone from her pocket and scrolled through her contacts. Since she only had Tate's cell phone number, she called the number for the house. Two rings later someone picked up.

"Hello."

Lena. The wife.

"Lena, hello, this is Brenda Devers."

"Brenda." She cleared her throat. "How are you and Janey?"

"We're getting through one day at a time. You and Trek okay?" Their son, Trek, was seven years old. Brenda could only imagine how difficult this was for him. Unlike Janey, who still thought her daddy would come back one day, Trek understood that was not the case.

"Fine. We're fine."

A strained silence stretched between them. Maybe she shouldn't have called.

"I was just wondering if you'd heard from the detective conducting the investigation into the explosion." Brenda held her breath.

She wasn't sure what she expected to get out of this conversation, but she'd needed to talk to someone else caught up in all this. Lena had lost her husband and the father of her child. They were in very similar boats. She and Lena hadn't become good friends as Brenda had initially expected they would. They spent time together whenever their husbands arranged some work thing disguised as a family get-together. Their kids played together well…but she and Lena never really hit it off. Now they were both widows—

Except Scott might not be dead… The victim in the office at the time of the explosion they had assumed was Scott was not him. Shock and defeat sucked at her, forcing her to lower into the nearest chair. The whole idea was insane.

"My attorney, Mr. Harris Carlisle," Lena began, then cleared her throat, "has advised me not to speak with you or anyone involved with the investigation."

Her attorney? "You have an attorney?"

"I'm… I'm sorry, Brenda. Please don't call me again."

The call ended. Brenda stared at the screen. Why would Lena's attorney advise her not to talk with Brenda? The office was jointly owned by Scott and Tate. It wasn't like Lena could sue Scott or his estate for damages any more than Brenda could sue Tate or his estate.

Unless she already knew that Scott wasn't dead and maybe the police now saw him as the primary suspect.

Brenda almost called her back, but she didn't. Instead, she called Detective Shelton.

"Shelton," he said rather than hello. The sound of traffic told her he was still on the road. Maybe headed home by now.

"Detective Shelton, this is Brenda Devers. I'm sorry to bother you but I just called Lena Jenner, and she said her attorney advised her not to talk to me. Do you have any idea why she would get that kind of advice? Scott and Tate were partners in the business and in the office. I can't imagine why she would see me as some sort of enemy." She just couldn't fathom what was going on.

A sigh hissed across the line. Brenda braced herself for news she obviously wasn't going to want to hear.

"Since your husband was not in the office at the time of the explosion, even though his car being in the parking lot and the fact that he told you he had a meeting there implied he was, it suggests…"

He didn't have to say the rest. "You think Scott arranged

for this man to be in the office and to die in his place." Dear God, there was no longer any way to ignore where this was going.

"There is no reason to believe otherwise," Shelton pointed out.

It was true then. The victim was a presumed setup and the detective believed Scott had arranged for him to be there.

"Why would he do that?" Brenda couldn't fathom the reason. Scott had life insurance, but how would that benefit him if he was supposed to be dead?

"There was a business policy in place. If anything happened to one or both partners, all debts and damages were covered. It appears," he said with audible reluctance, "the business was in deep financial trouble."

"What? No. He bought a house last year. How could he be in financial trouble?"

"The house on The Ledges," Shelton said, "was leased. Not purchased."

A new wave of shock radiated through her. Brenda didn't know what to say. "Okay," she finally managed to get out. "Scott and Tate were partners. If the business was in trouble, that would involve both of them." She couldn't stop thinking about how Lena refused to speak with her…had retained an attorney. A big-deal attorney at that.

"Ms. Devers, the bottom line is that your husband, Scott," Shelton explained, "is no longer a victim in this investigation."

Her breath left her in a rush as the reality of the situation sank fully in. "He's a suspect." The words croaked out of her, no matter that she had known this was coming.

"Yes."

"Who was the other man—the one I buried." This was too much.

"We don't know yet," Shelton explained. "But you should be aware that given this latest turn of events, we'll be applying for a warrant to search your home, Ms. Devers. Your bank accounts will be frozen."

"Wait, we've been separated for a year. We each have our own bank account." This was not right.

"The two of you were still married. There's not a lot more I can tell you, Brenda." That he used her first name had her going cold. "My advice? Go to an ATM and take out as much cash as you can as quickly as you can."

The call ended and Brenda simply sat there for a time. This had to be wrong. A mistake of some sort. Why would Scott kill his partner and arrange for someone else to die in his own place? Was he trying to outmaneuver their creditors? Surely they weren't mixed up with loan sharks. It was ridiculous to even think…

No matter how she analyzed what she had just learned, the truth was Brenda knew nothing of Scott's business dealings. He did his thing and she did hers when it came to careers. She was aware his company was an investment firm, but she had no idea about the details or the clients. In fact, she actually knew very little about Scott's partner, Tate. Or his wife. She just assumed…too much apparently.

She had made a terrible, terrible mistake allowing herself to be so oblivious.

Chapter Four

5:45 p.m.

A knock on her door had Brenda lunging to her feet.

The pizza must have been delivered. She went to the door and opened it.

But instead of her new neighbor there was another man. Older. Fortyish. His navy suit was rumpled, and he needed a shave. A few threads of gray had found their way through his dark hair.

"Ms. Devers?"

She glanced at the briefcase he carried. "Yes."

He removed a credentials case from a pocket in his jacket and opened it to reveal a photo ID. "I'm Special Agent Jarrod Cummings with the FBI. May I have a few moments of your time?"

Ben appeared behind him, pizza boxes in hand. He looked from the man standing between them to Brenda. "Hello. Pizza's here."

Cummings turned slightly, glancing at the man who had walked up behind him. The agent stepped aside and allowed Ben to pass.

Brenda wasn't sure what to say to either man.

"I'll just take these to the kitchen," Ben suggested.

She nodded, relieved to have one dilemma solved. When he'd gone into the kitchen, she looked to the agent. "I'm sorry. I just arrived home from a cross-country business trip. I'm exhausted and my child is hungry. Can you leave a card, and we can do this tomorrow?"

Sounded reasonable to Brenda.

The man's head moved slowly up and down as if he were considering her request rather than responding to it. Finally, he replied, "Sure." He dug around in his pocket and produced a business card. "Call as early as possible," he said. "This is a pressing matter."

She accepted the card. "Can you tell me what it's about?" The last thing she wanted to do was spend the night wondering.

"Your husband, Scott Devers."

She wilted a little. What had she expected?

When the man walked away, she closed the door and sagged against it. What in the world? This was like something from one of her books. Only she hadn't written the premise and had no clue what was coming.

Janey's sweet little voice echoed from the kitchen. Brenda pushed away from the door and drifted in that direction. Her little girl sat on a stool at the island, munching on pizza, Ben next to her.

"Mommy, it's good." Janey grabbed another slice.

Brenda smiled. "Smells delicious."

"I took the liberty," her neighbor said as he tapped the bottle of wine Brenda had only just then noticed. Two stemmed glasses sat next to it. "I thought maybe you might want to celebrate. Mallory told me the movie deal was a go."

Whether he knew it or not, he had chosen her favorite chardonnay. She might just hug the guy. "That would be so, so good right now."

He opened the bottle and poured her and himself a glass. Brenda ate, realizing that the alcohol would go straight to her head if she didn't eat first. Janey talked and munched, talked and munched. Mallory's comment about their neighbor obviously hadn't put the child off and, thankfully, she didn't repeat it.

Half an hour later, Janey proclaimed she was stuffed, and about that same time the grandfather clock counted off seven slow, deep dongs.

The child's eyes went wide. "It's time for my show!"

"First," Brenda argued, "we wash hands." She picked Janey up and took her to the sink to wash her face and hands. "Now you can watch your show, then it's bedtime."

As soon as Janey was on her feet, she rushed to the sofa and grabbed the remote. She knew how to turn the TV on and the proper channel to select. Brenda didn't allow her to watch a lot of television, only her favorites.

"You seem unsettled," Ben said when her attention shifted back to him. "Everything okay?" He shook his head. "I understand everything is not all right with all that's happened. But is there something new? I thought you'd be celebrating."

She eased onto a stool, her body and soul feeling heavy. "It has been a bizarre day." Other than Mallory, Brenda really had no one to talk to. There was her agent, but she resisted the urge to talk with a work colleague about her personal life, especially the not-so-good parts. For the past six years she'd been totally absorbed in Scott's world as far as socializing went, and that had dwindled until it was nonexistent. On top of that, having Janey had occupied so much of her time that between writing and being a mommy, she really had no time for socializing anyway. Mallory was always a good sounding board, but she was also biased. She thought Scott was a scumbag and that Brenda was an angel for putting up with him. Apparently he was.

Not to mention he was apparently alive.

Anger lit in her belly. They'd had a memorial service for him. Buried the remains of some stranger in the newly purchased plot at Maple Hill Cemetery.

So yes, he was a scumbag.

"Well." She picked up her wineglass and drank deeply, then wiped her mouth.

Why not spill her guts to this man? They didn't know each other. He was new in the neighborhood and appeared to be a bit of a loner, like her, so it wasn't likely he would be telling anyone. At least not anyone she knew.

"I was in LAX today, and I could have sworn I saw him. Scott, my husband," she clarified. "But I felt like a fool because—" she shrugged "—he's dead. I buried him nearly three weeks ago. Then I came home, and the detective who has been investigating the explosion showed up and told me that the man I buried was not my husband. In other words, Scott isn't dead. At least, if he is, he wasn't killed by the explosion."

Ben frowned. "But his body was found..."

Brenda shook her head. "No. That body belonged to someone else. DNA confirmed it wasn't Scott." She made a face that said *I think I'm losing it*. "So maybe I did see him at LAX today all hugged up with a tall, leggy blonde."

She pressed her fingers to her lips. She hadn't meant to say that last part.

"Wow." Ben's eyebrows reared up. "That's a hell of a day you've had."

"How could he be alive?" She moved her head side to side and stared at the stranger eating pizza and drinking wine in her kitchen. "I have known Scott for nearly seven years. He has been—more often than not—a bit of an arrogant…" She drew in a deep breath, then took another healthy swallow of wine. "Anyway, his business has always been very important to him. His partner and associates more important than his family, it seemed at times. Why would he do this? I mean, I have to assume—or at least the police do—that he set up the explosion."

Brenda laughed out loud at her own words, then her fingers went back to her lips. Oh God, she should stop talking. No laughing either.

"So, he's a suspect now," Ben offered.

She nodded. Shelton had said that. "Which means, I think, that he's suspected of having arranged the explosion and faking his death—killing three people in the process."

"Did the detective offer a motive, or do you know of any reason Scott might do such a thing?"

The question was so calm. His eyes—really sweet eyes—showed genuine concern. If her judgment could be trusted, and she didn't have a stellar record so far.

"Shelton—the detective—said the business was in serious financial trouble." She thought about that for a moment. "Since it's an investment firm, I'm assuming trouble means client money is missing." Which also meant that everything Scott owned outright or jointly would be on the chopping block. Apprehension slid through her. "I need to go to an ATM."

He looked surprised. "Can it wait until morning?"

She shook her head. "Shelton said they would probably freeze all assets and accounts."

"I see." He thought for a moment, then offered, "Why don't we let Janey watch her show, and then I'll drive you to the ATM."

"I could walk," she argued. "It's just down the street."

"Probably not a good idea since the bank is closed."

He had a valid point. Five Points was a great neighborhood, but that bank had been robbed numerous times. It was one of those strange enigmas. "If you're sure you don't mind."

"I do not mind at all."

Brenda closed up the leftover pizza and started to clean up. She had to think about all this. It was unbelievable. And she needed to do something rather than sit here and puzzle over the insanity.

"Do you have any family you can call?" he asked as he wiped off the island with a damp paper towel.

The question startled her, but it was a fair one. He didn't know her. He had no idea if she had family or friends or whatever.

"No. There's no one but me and Janey."

"What about Scott? Does he have any family you might be able to contact? Maybe they've heard from him."

"No one. At least no one I know about." Suddenly everything Scott had ever told her was in question. "He said his parents were deceased and he had no siblings—just like me. Our only friends were his work friends, my literary agent and Mallory." She managed a smile that was likely pretty pitiful. "How sad is that?"

"Busy people don't always have time for all the usual social trappings."

She paused as she put the lid back on the wine. "The man who was here when you arrived with the pizza was from the FBI."

This new twist was very bad. Really bad. She didn't need a law degree to see that. The FBI didn't investigate low-level local crime… This had to be something far bigger than she dared to suspect.

Ben lifted one shoulder in a vague shrug. "Not surprising in Scott's line of work. Embezzling, money laundering would likely warrant the involvement of the federal authorities."

She closed her eyes a moment. Good grief, he was right. "Money laundering. I never even thought of that. So, he might be involved with criminal people or entities."

This was really, really bad. Money laundering involved concealing the illegal and criminal origins of funds and transferring those funds around in legal accounts, foreign and/or domestic, in order to make them appear legitimate. Bad, bad business.

"If that's the case," her neighbor confirmed, "then yes."

"We're still married, but my financial assets were mine before we married. This house was mine before we married. Will any of those things be up for grabs?" This was a true nightmare. An even bigger one than she could have conceived, and that was saying something considering her line of work.

"A good attorney should be able to ensure whatever was yours before the marriage is set aside. Perhaps you're borrowing trouble. You don't actually know what the problem is just yet. It may be something far less worrisome for you."

She settled back on a stool, rested her elbows on the countertop and plopped her chin in her hands. "It has to be bad. Otherwise, why fake his death?"

"You were separated, correct?"

"Yes. For a year now, but he was in no hurry to sign the divorce papers or to agree to any sort of custody terms."

"He was buying time."

Brenda hadn't thought of that. Though she couldn't imagine why he would want or need to buy time. "Maybe."

"Since his supposed death, have you noticed anyone new

or different coming around at the places you shop or frequent? In the neighborhood?"

She thought about that for a bit, then shook her head. "No. Not until the FBI agent today." Her gaze narrowed. "Except you." She laughed, a weary sound. "You're new and right next door."

He laughed as well. "I am. But you needn't be concerned with me."

"Do you think I could find anything on the internet? About Scott or his business?"

"You can look," he agreed. "I'm guessing the authorities won't have released anything significant, and if your husband was smart, he will have kept his illegal business dealings on the down-low."

Well, of course he would.

If only she had a contact in law enforcement. She'd interviewed the community liaison officer of the local department plenty of times. But she doubted he would have access to the sort of information she would need. Another thought suddenly occurred to her, igniting a new terror in her.

She looked to her neighbor. "Do you think Janey and I are in danger? I mean, if he did this to escape trouble...how can I be sure his trouble won't come after us?"

"You can't. But if no one has come around before today, then chances are they believed he was dead. The real issue will be when word gets out that he's not."

Something else she hadn't thought of.

"I do need an attorney," she realized aloud. "Maybe personal security and a private investigator." Now she actually did sound like a character from one of her novels.

"I can't argue with you," Ben said. "This could be something the police will resolve fairly quickly, but it could still be dangerous for anyone who was close to him."

She knew no attorneys—at least, not criminal attorneys. Not once, even for a second, had she ever dreamed she would need one. And her new neighbor wasn't from the area so she doubted he would know anyone local who could navigate this sort of situation. But she did know people. Like the mayor. Several high-level local government officials she had interviewed for research. She would talk to them. Surely one or the other would have suggestions.

She tensed. "He said—Detective Shelton—that he had requested a warrant for searching my house. I guess they already searched Scott's." The one he didn't own, the liar.

"Do you have reason to believe he would have hidden anything here?"

"No." She shook her head. "He was rarely even here over the past year."

"Did he have a key?"

The question gave her pause. "He did—does. Of course. We have Janey, and sometimes he would bring her home to pick up something on his weekend. If I wasn't here he would let himself in."

"Then you can't be sure he didn't leave something that might cause difficulty for you during a search by the police."

God, he was right. "I should search the house."

"The sooner the better," he suggested.

She blew out a big breath. "Thanks for the pizza and the…" She shrugged. "For being a good listener, but I have a lot to do before I call it a night, to include taking this place apart."

"You should and you're welcome."

She followed him to the door. "Really, thank you, for listening."

He flashed her a smile. "Some people just make that sort of thing easy."

Chapter Five

Wednesday, May 6
Devers Residence
White Street
Huntsville, 3:20 a.m.

Brenda roused. Her eyes drifted open. The room was dark… the house quiet. A frown furrowed across her brow, tugging at her senses. What time was it?

She shifted slightly, just enough to see the digital clock on her bedside table. 3:21 a.m. Too early. Her eyes closed and she burrowed more deeply into her covers. Listened to the wind swaying a limb that scrubbed the side of the house. *Scratch. Scratch.* She really needed to get that limb trimmed.

A click, then the almost imperceptible slide of something… maybe a shoe…a footstep…whispered through the darkness…

Her eyes flew open again. Her body went stone-still. She held her breath. Listened. Had she imagined it…fallen asleep and dreamed it? Another faint swish of sound…a clink of metal or glass.

Janey? Had she gotten out of bed and gone to the bathroom?

Brenda swept the cover from her body and eased upward, cringing at the soft sigh of the sheets sliding apart. If Janey was asleep, she definitely wanted her to stay that way. Her feet settled on the cool hardwood floor, and she pushed up to a standing position. Her bones settled, her muscles coming to attention as her mind brushed away the last remnants of sleep. She threaded her fingers through her hair, dragging it out of her eyes. The silence thickened around her. Maybe she had been dreaming…

Another swish made her freeze.

A whine echoed then…the sort of sound her daughter made when she didn't want to wake up but something or someone had disturbed her.

Brenda's breath caught.

A cry pierced the air.

"Mommy!" Janey sobbed.

Brenda bolted from her bedroom, her heart pounding like a drum, keeping a triple tick with the sound of her child's distress.

"Coming, sweetie!"

Her body came to a jarring halt against an unyielding object…something out of place. For a moment Brenda couldn't assimilate what had occurred. Something big and solid, like an unexpected wall, had stopped her.

Brenda drew slightly back, blinked at the blackness… then something shifted and a pair of eyes turned toward hers.

Fear rammed into her throat, trapping a scream there.

Strong hands shoved her against the wall. She tumbled sideways, landing on the floor. Framed photographs rattled; at least one skated down the wall and hit the floor with a cracking sound.

A swoosh of movement…rapid footfalls.

A scream pierced the air.

Janey.

Brenda scrambled to her feet.

A loud thud reverberated through the house. But her only concern at the moment was for her daughter.

Brenda didn't dare turn on a light. She couldn't be sure if the intruder had left or was still in the house. She flung herself through the door to Janey's room, slammed it shut and locked it.

She fell to her knees next to the bed, grabbed her sobbing child and wrapped her in her arms. Pressed her lips to her hair and softly shushed her.

Then she listened, held her breath in an attempt to hear above the hammering in her chest…the roaring of blood in her ears.

Quiet…nothing.

Scrape...scrape.

Wait! Another surge of adrenaline fired through her.

Brenda held perfectly still, listened.

Scrape...scrape. The wind…and that damned tree limb. She relaxed the tiniest bit.

Maybe it was over now… That loud thud may have been a door. Brenda forced her brain to think, to analyze the situation.

Someone had been inside the house…shoved her to the floor.

"Janey," she whispered, "I need you to hide while I see if it's safe now."

"Noooo," her baby whimpered. She snuggled closer to her mother.

"We have to call the police," Brenda whispered. "I need my phone." She should have picked it up when she got out of bed. What had she been thinking?

Certainly not about an intruder. Only that she needed to get up and check on her child.

"It's in my room. I'll be right back for you."

"I'm scared," Janey cried.

Brenda stood, holding her daughter close against her, and crossed the room. She opened the door to the closet and lowered to her knees. She settled Janey on the floor at the back of the small space.

"You stay in here. Don't come out for anything. I'll be back to get you in just a minute, okay?"

Her daughter nodded fearfully, tears running down her cheeks.

Pushing back to her feet, Brenda closed the door. She stretched her neck. Squared her shoulders and walked to the bedroom door.

She closed her eyes and listened. Nothing. Not even the wind. She reached out, touched the knob…released the button lock. Deep breath. She opened the door.

Blackness greeted her. But no sound…no solid body…no eyes. A shiver raced through her. Was he gone?

Hopefully.

She walked into the hall and started toward her bedroom, listening intently. With every step, she moved more quickly. When she at last had her phone in her hand she entered the necessary numbers.

"9-1-1, what is the nature of your emergency?" the voice on the phone said, sending some small measure of relief through her.

"I woke to an intruder in the house," Brenda explained as she walked to the third bedroom, poked her head through the open door and glanced around as best she could without turning on the light. If he was still outside or nearby somewhere she didn't want him to see lights coming on. Was that the right thing to do? She wasn't sure. "My name is Brenda

Devers." She recited her address in answer to the call taker's question. Then she moved on toward the living room.

"Are you safe, Ms. Devers?"

"Yes. I think so. He appears to be gone but I'm not sure. My four-year-old daughter and I are here alone."

The call taker assured Brenda that a pair of officers were already en route and should arrive within five minutes. Brenda was to stay on the line.

"Thank you." Brenda drew in a deep breath for the first time since hearing the sound of her child whimpering.

While she waited, she checked the living room and kitchen and under the table in the dining nook. Maybe she'd been half asleep and tripped and fell. Maybe the whole thing had been a nightmare and… The back door stood open. She stiffened. Not a nightmare. Not her imagination. It was real then. There had been someone in the house. Several emotions swam through her veins. Fear…anger…affirmation.

"Are you armed, Ms. Devers?"

The voice startled her no matter that Brenda still had the phone pressed to her ear. "No," she said, clearing her head of the thoughts tugging her in a dozen directions.

"Is there a firearm in the house?"

"No." Brenda turned around and around in the center of her kitchen. *Someone had been in her house.* And she was unarmed. Her husband had been the one with the handgun. He'd taken it with him when he moved out—after his last round of cheating. After ripping apart the final tatters of their relationship.

He is alive.

The realization rattled her. The explosion…three dead… DNA…an attorney for the Jenners. The horrors flooded in like a lake spilling over a dam.

"Looks like the, ah…" She swallowed in hopes of dampening her dry throat. "The intruder came in and then left through the back door." She forced the other worries away. Had to focus. "It's standing open." Maybe the thud she heard had been him running into something.

"Stay inside," the call taker warned. "The officers are approaching your home now."

The news set her in motion. Brenda hurried back to her daughter's room and opened the closet door. She reached in and pulled a shivering Janey into her arms. "It's okay, baby. We're safe now."

But were they?

No way. Something was going on with Scott and whatever trouble his firm had gotten involved with. She and Janey might never be safe again.

A couple of sharp raps against the front door were followed by, "Huntsville Police!"

Practically running, Brenda rushed to the door and opened it. The sight of the two uniformed officers made her weep. The tears hit her so hard and fast…so unexpectedly that she couldn't remain standing. She collapsed to the floor, Janey hugged against her chest.

One officer moved past and headed into the house, turning on lights as he went. The other crouched down and surveyed her. "Are you all right, ma'am? Do you need medical attention?"

"No." She swiped at her eyes. "I'm fine. I'm sorry. I just…" She shook her head. Couldn't explain the sudden eruption of emotions.

"It's all right." He stood, held out a hand. "Let's get you and your daughter over to the couch, and then I'll have a look around outside."

She took his hand, her relief so profound she couldn't

hold back another surge of tears. She felt so foolish. She never broke down like this.

When he'd ushered her onto the sofa, he walked back outside. She watched beyond the window as his flashlight moved over the yard…over the shrubs that had bloomed so beautifully last year and were showing signs of the same this year. This was her and Janey's home. Their private space… their safe place. Emotion clogged her throat once more and she fought it back. She couldn't keep falling apart like this. Janey needed her to be strong. She was watching, taking her cues from her mother. Brenda had to keep it together better than this.

Shouting outside had her hunkering lower on the sofa. Janey whimpered. "Shh, shh. It's okay." Brenda surely hoped it was okay.

The officer who had helped her to the sofa appeared at the front door once more. "Ma'am, there's a Ben Clark out here. He says he's your neighbor."

The officer who'd gone deeper into her home came from the direction of the bedrooms. "All clear," he said to his partner.

Brenda nodded to the officer at her door. "Yes. Ben Clark is my neighbor."

"He wants to see you, but it's best if no one else comes into the house until we're finished."

Brenda somehow managed to get to her feet. "Is it okay if my daughter and I go next door and stay until you need us?"

"Yes, ma'am. My partner will be over to take your statement once we've completed the assessment of the situation here."

Brenda nodded and headed out the door. Ben waited on the sidewalk.

"Are you two okay?"

Brenda managed another deep breath. "Yes. We're… fine."

He ushered the two of them along the sidewalk to the gate that opened into his front yard. By the time they were walking through his door, Brenda's heart rate had reached some semblance of normalcy and Janey had stopped sobbing.

"Sit anywhere you like," he suggested as he closed and locked the door.

Brenda settled onto the sofa and finally drew Janey back so she could see her face. "You okay, baby?"

Janey nodded, her dark hair hanging like a disheveled curtain around her face. Brenda smoothed and pushed it away. "We're okay now," she promised.

"You need coffee?" Ben asked. "Hot chocolate?"

Janey came to life then. "Hot chocolate," she enthused. She slid out of her mother's lap and hurried to the man, grabbed him by the hand and peered up at him. "You have marshmallows?"

He smiled. "I do." He glanced at Brenda then. "Anything for you?"

She shook her head. Nothing short of a shot of whiskey was going to give her one iota of comfort just now.

When Ben had taken Janey to the kitchen, Brenda closed her eyes and fought back the images and thoughts that wanted to haunt her. Right now, she needed to get her wits about her. No more tears. No more moments of weakness. The sound of Janey's sweet little girl voice and Ben's far deeper one made her smile. Thank God for this new neighbor.

Minutes, maybe a half hour, later—Brenda couldn't say for sure but long enough that Janey was asking for another cup with extra marshmallows—a rap on the door snapped her to attention. She slipped into that neutral place where she didn't have to think about all the what-ifs and whys.

She stood and headed for the door. "I've got it," she called to Ben, who appeared at the cased opening between the living room and kitchen.

"We're having seconds in here," he told her. "Still nothing for you?"

"No thanks. Can you keep Janey in the kitchen?" She didn't want her daughter to overhear whatever the officers had to report.

"Of course."

Ben turned back to the kitchen, and Brenda opened the front door. Only one officer waited there. "Did you find anything?" she asked, keeping her voice lowered no matter that she wanted to shout.

"Is it all right if I come inside?"

"Oh, yes." Brenda shook her head. "Forgive me."

When they'd settled in the living room, her on the sofa once more and the officer in a side chair opposite her, he answered her question. "We believe the intruder started in the garage and worked his way to the house."

The garage was at the back of her house where a narrow alley provided off-street parking for homeowners. Not all had garages, but both hers and the house next door did.

She nodded for him to go on, her arms instinctively wrapping around herself.

"Boxes and containers you have stored there were overturned and dug around in. Looks like your car was searched. Glove box contents are on the floorboard. Trunk was open."

"Good grief, what on earth could anyone have been looking for in my car?" She didn't leave any change or cash lying around in her car and certainly nothing else of value inside.

"Unless something is missing," the officer explained

as he took out a pad and pen, "it's difficult to determine what he was looking for. But we believe when he didn't find what he was looking for in the garage, he moved on to the house. The yard and patio area appear pretty much undisturbed other than the overturning of flowerpots. In the house, my partner found drawers partially opened, and the books and items on shelves were moved aside, some placed on the floor. The search in the house was fairly thorough."

Her jaw dropped and she shook her head. "How could I sleep through that?" And why hadn't she noticed open drawers or anything else? Maybe because she hadn't turned on any lights, just poked her head through the door of her office. As foolish as it seemed now, before the police arrived the darkness had felt like a cloak of protection preventing anyone from seeing her through the windows. Keeping her movements secret.

"If he was a professional then he knew how to look without making noise. It's obvious in the garage that he didn't care, but he was far more careful inside. The drawers were only partially open, as if he wanted his efforts not to be noticeable but didn't want to risk the sound of fully closing them."

"Still, I can't believe he went all through the house and wasn't afraid of waking me."

"Like I said," the officer reiterated, "looks like a professional job. Can you recall anything about him? Height? Weight? Gloves? Mask? Anything at all?"

This was so over-the-top...so surreal. Why was this happening? Brenda pushed all the troubling thoughts aside. "He was tall, a good deal taller than me."

"So maybe close to six feet?"

She nodded. "Solid. Muscled. His hands were really strong. And yes, he was wearing gloves. Black...all black.

It was like he wasn't even there, but then I saw his eyes. He was wearing a ski-type mask of some sort. All I saw were his eyes. They were maybe blue or gray. Lighter in color. It happened really fast and I was startled so I can't be sure."

"That's good," he assured her. "Really good." He made a few more notes.

"I guess I should look around and see if he took anything." Surely he hadn't been in her room with her asleep in the bed. She had a few pieces of jewelry that were fairly valuable. But most of what she owned carried only sentimental value.

"You should, yes. But—" his gaze connected fully with hers "—we don't think this was a typical robbery."

A frown tugged at her lips. "What do you mean?"

"There was jewelry in your bedroom. Cash in your handbag. A laptop and iPad in your office. Not to mention your cell phone. None of that was taken. Also, you have some pain medication in your medicine cabinet."

She nodded, remembering Scott's accident on the racquetball court last summer. "My husband fractured his ankle. They sent him home with pain meds, but he never took them." She should have dropped them off at a disposal center already.

The officer held up a hand. "I understand. My point is there were a lot of things he could have taken for readily converting to cash but didn't. Do you have any reason to believe someone would be looking for anything in particular in your home?"

She moved her head side to side. "No. I'm a writer, but I'm far from rich. I don't have anything, not one thing I would call valuable for someone looking to make quick cash—except the things you already named."

"I ask because..." He picked up his cell phone, tapped the

screen then turned it toward her. "This was spray-painted on the interior of your garage door."

WHERE IS IT?

Her breath escaped her in a rush. "I… I have no idea what that means." She lifted her gaze to the officer's. "I can only assume it's about my husband."

"Does your husband not live here with you?" he asked. "And do you have reason to believe he, or someone associated with him, may have been the intruder who came into your home tonight?"

Brenda moistened her lips. "Officer…" She looked at his name tag. "Officer Grayson, just a couple of weeks ago I buried what I believed were my husband's remains." At his look of confusion she went on. "Until yesterday I've spent the better part of a month believing he was dead."

Grayson readied his pen above his notepad. "Let's start at the beginning," he suggested. "From when you first woke up and heard the intruder. When we have tonight's ordeal down, we'll talk about your husband."

Brenda glanced toward the kitchen, where Ben and Janey were still happily ensconced around the island. What in the world was happening to their lives?

What had Scott gotten them into?

Chapter Six

9:30 a.m.

Brenda stared at the words painted on the inside of her garage door.

WHERE IS IT?

This was over-the-top…completely mad.

The police had dusted for prints in her house and garage. Brenda and Janey had provided theirs to narrow down the numerous impressions taken. Detective Shelton had arrived at seven. He had informed the officers that Scott's prints had already been lifted from his home on The Ledges, which would provide further elimination of the many taken from her home.

Shelton had questioned her again about Scott. But she knew nothing that she hadn't already shared. Well, except the story about thinking she had seen him in Los Angeles. Considering the DNA results and then this break-in, she had told the detective about the strange encounter at LAX. She suspected, based on his reaction, that she hadn't helped her case with the news. If he hadn't already thought she was guilty of something, he surely thought so now. His suggestion that her trip to Los Angeles was about meeting Scott rather than about her writing had infuriated her.

The idea that she hadn't told him from the start would forever be suspicious in his opinion.

Finally, about half an hour ago, all the Huntsville PD personnel, including Shelton, had packed up and left. Brenda wanted to feel glad they were gone, but right now all she felt was confused. Mallory had arrived as they were leaving. Brenda had called her and explained the situation. She couldn't come to work at her usual time of eight with the police still working.

Now, Brenda only wanted to call a housekeeper. She generally took care of her own housekeeping and laundry, but this mess was overwhelming. Not to mention she felt the need to sanitize the whole house considering a stranger had gone through it—had touched their things. Then the police had done the same. Mallory had taken one look around and offered to help, but Brenda just wanted to order a bulldozer.

The garage was even worse. She and Ben had come to have a firsthand look to better assess the situation. Unbelievably, even her Christmas tree and decorations had been dumped on the floor.

Ben turned to her—they had both been staring at the graffiti for the past minute or so. "I can cover this if you have paint."

"I think I do. Somewhere around here." She studied him for a moment, doubts assaulting her. "That really would be above and beyond the call for a new neighbor."

He chuckled. "I grew up on a farm in rural Illinois. Trust me, this is what good neighbors, new or old, do."

It was more likely that he was feeling sorry for her. Last night after he'd gone home, she had to call and ask for a ride to the bank. He'd said he would take her but then she'd forgotten. She'd had at least one too many glasses of wine to drive herself. So he'd taken her to the bank to use the ATM and then he'd stayed at her house for a little while after Janey fell back to sleep, and Brenda had spilled her guts about Scott...how their relationship ended and every other dirty detail of the past six years. That was what happened after too many glasses of wine and way too much stress.

She couldn't help feeling a little embarrassed now. But, frankly, it was difficult to hold on to any emotions for long at the moment. They kept changing. One minute she was as mad as hell. The next she wanted to weep. Then she moved on to total numbness. Through it all these threads of suspicion lingered...wove around and inside her like an out-of-control, suffocating vine.

What had Scott been doing? When had it started?

And who was this really nice guy named Ben Clark?

"What I need," she said, pushing the thought away as this new idea came to her in a rush, "is time to figure this out. To determine what sort of mess Scott has left us with."

Ben nodded. "That's a good idea. I'm confident Detective Shelton will do all he can to solve the mystery of the explosion and your husband's strange disappearance, but a second look from a different perspective never hurts."

She took a breath. "I agree. Just one thing."

He stared at her expectantly.

"I'd like to stop referring to him as my husband. We've been separated for a year. The only thing that defined us as husband and wife was a legal document we signed years ago. Obviously the problems I knew about were just the tip of the iceberg. Calling him my husband feels too intimate, and we hadn't been intimate in any way in a very long time." Maybe she'd said too much. Her cheeks flushed. "Sorry... I'm not myself."

"Completely understandable." He gave her a nod. "No more use of the *H* word."

She felt a smile tug at her lips. Brenda had no idea how this man—this stranger—managed to prod that out of her. She had absolutely nothing to smile about.

"Before we jump into full Sherlock Holmes mode," he suggested, "I think we should make breakfast."

Mallory had likely already made breakfast for Janey. Brenda's stomach warned she had ignored eating too often lately. "Breakfast first." She hesitated, scrutinized his face once more. "We?" she asked. "Don't you have work or something better to do than to dig around in this mess with me?"

"My office is wherever I am," he explained. "I work on my own schedule, so whenever anything comes up, it's easy for me to rearrange my agenda."

For a single second a new drip of suspicion trickled through her.

She opted to face it head-on. "I don't think you ever told me what you do."

Under the circumstances, no one could blame her for this new stream of uncertainty. It was coming on the heels of weeks of personal upheaval complicated by an intruder. Who could blame her for suddenly needing to know more about anyone new to her life? Her respiration quickened, sending her heart into a faster rhythm. What if she was standing right here with the man who'd come into her house last night? He lived next door… He knew a lot about her and her home.

Slow down, Brenda. She drew in a deep breath. *Give the man a chance to answer.*

"Research," he said. "I interview people. Watch people and report my findings. I can't discuss my clients with you. But I can tell you that I study all sorts of human behaviors and human nature. I write reports and submit them." He shrugged. "It's not glamorous but it's important for my clients."

That he remained so patient and so kind she couldn't help feeling contrite for questioning him. Paranoia had obviously crept up on her. "Sorry. I've just had a little extra uncertainty thrown into my life, and I'm feeling a little lacking in the trust area."

"You can trust me, Brenda." He said the words gently, sincerely. "I have no reason to want to deceive you or to harm you."

Brenda suddenly wondered how long it would take for her to stop using all the promises Scott had broken…all the lies he had told her as a gauge to measure other men—people in general, for that matter.

"Come on," he urged. "Breakfast first, then I'll paint."

Back in the house, Mallory sat on the floor of Janey's room surrounded by Barbie dolls. Brenda had no idea how she had been lucky enough to find Mallory, but she was sincerely grateful for her. Janey adored her. Considering how absent Scott was even before his fake death, Mallory was a lifesaver. Both Brenda and Janey had been close to Leah, the first nanny Brenda had hired. Two years ago, when she died in a car crash, they had been devastated. After losing Leah, quite honestly Brenda had worried about hiring anyone else. To have Janey get so close to someone and then to lose that person, it was worrisome. When she'd dared to interview Mallory, there were no more questions. She was perfect.

Now her child had gone through losing a parent—who wasn't really dead as it turned out. How would Brenda ever make Janey understand this? One thing was certain. She would not even broach the subject until—unless—he was back in person.

If that ever happened. Brenda shook her head. At this point it was impossible to even guess what was coming next.

When Brenda turned to head back to the kitchen, Ben held up a hand. "Spend time with your daughter," he urged. "I'll take care of breakfast."

Brenda didn't argue. Once again, she was too exhausted to muster up the effort. Instead, she and Mallory played like little girls with Janey. Before Brenda realized how much time had passed, Ben was calling them to the kitchen. Although Mallory had microwaved a waffle for Janey, the child was hungry for more.

Crispy bacon, scrambled eggs and buttered toast. Fresh fruit and yogurt.

"Looks yummy," Brenda confessed. Smelled even yummier.

She suspected Ben had gotten the bacon from his kitchen. She was pretty sure her supply was nonexistent, as she hadn't had a chance to go to the store since her return from LA. Mallory poured the orange juice while Ben made fresh coffee. Brenda felt relaxed for the first time since before she went to Los Angeles. It wouldn't last, she suspected. But she intended to enjoy it as long as possible.

When Ben stepped out onto the back patio to take a call, Mallory leaned across the island. "Is this guy for real?" Her green eyes twinkled with laughter.

Brenda shrugged. "He's really nice."

Mallory devoured a slice of bacon. "Makes you wonder if cooking is the only thing he's so good at?"

Brenda shot her a look as the back door opened and the man in question walked in once more.

"This breakfast is really good," Brenda said, hoping to cover anything he might have heard. "Thank you so much, Ben."

"See," Janey piped up, "I told you he wasn't strange. Ben is nice." She beamed a smile at him as he resumed his seat next to Brenda.

Brenda bit her lips together and hoped he wouldn't catch on.

Mallory coughed as if a piece of bacon had gone down the wrong way.

Ben laughed and fluttered his hands on either side of his head as he leaned closer to Janey. "I can be very strange, little girl. Want to see?"

"No," Janey squealed, then melted into giggles.

"I was only saying," Mallory stammered, "that it's better to be careful of strangers."

"Very good advice," Ben said to Janey. "You should listen to Mallory. She's smart." He shot the nanny a wink.

Mallory blushed.

Brenda scooted off her stool. "Since Ben cooked," she announced, "Mallory and I will clean up." She grabbed her plate and glass and headed to the sink. As she passed Ben, she teased, "Ben has Barbie duty."

"Yay," Janey cheered.

Mallory joined Brenda at the sink, and they struggled not to burst into giggles. The moment of relief was one Brenda was enormously grateful for.

After working in silence for a few minutes, Brenda loaded the last of the silverware into the dishwasher and closed the door. "I wanted to talk to you privately for a few minutes."

Mallory leaned against the counter and dried her hands. "Sure." She gave a humorless laugh. "I won't even ask what you want to talk about."

Brenda rolled her eyes. "No kidding."

Then she took a moment to steel herself. This was more than a little difficult for her, but it was the right thing to do.

As soon as she'd recovered from waking to that intruder, she had known what she had to do.

"I'm worried that it isn't safe for Janey to be here until we figure this out." There, she'd said it.

Surprise flashed across Mallory's face, but it passed quickly. "You're right. As difficult as it is to view the situation that way, I don't believe either of you are safe."

Brenda shrugged. "Probably not, but I'm the adult. I need to try and make it safe again. And the only way to do that is for me to figure out what it is that Scott has gotten us into and try to straighten it out."

Mallory tossed the hand towel aside. "Can't the police do that?"

"I'm sure they can," Brenda admitted, "in time. But I can't risk waiting. I need to find answers. The police are overworked, and they don't know Scott the way I do." She laughed. "Well, given everything I've learned in the last twenty-four hours or so, maybe I don't really know him either. But the things I do know could make a difference. Bottom line, I can't just sit around and wait. I need to find answers. Fast. Lena Jenner has already retained an attorney. Someone has searched my home. This is going to crash and burn around us—sooner rather than later, I fear. I don't want to be the person sitting around waiting for someone else to do what needs to be done."

"But you can't do this alone," Mallory urged. "It's not safe."

"Ben wants to help me."

Mallory's expression turned apprehensive. "But you don't really know this man. He's nice and all…but he is a stranger."

"Don't worry," she assured the other woman. "I will find out what I need to know first. But I have to do this."

"I understand." Mallory nodded. "To be honest, I am more than a little worried about Janey's safety in particular. She is exactly what the bad guys would go after if they wanted to hurt or pressure you."

The most terrifying aspect of what Mallory had just said was that it was true. "I know, that's what scares me."

"Just tell me what you need from me," Mallory insisted. "You know I will do whatever I can."

Relief and, at the same time, new worry plagued Brenda. But she had to do this.

"I need you to take Janey somewhere that *this*, whatever it is, can't touch her. If you and Peter can get the time away, I will gladly pay for a vacation to someplace where Janey will be safe." Peter was like Brenda—he worked from home so taking time away from an office wasn't an issue.

"You don't have to do that," Mallory argued. "We can take her to the cabin in Gatlinburg. My mother is always complaining that no one goes there enough anymore."

"Oh wow, that would be great." Brenda hadn't even thought of the cabin.

Mallory reached out, gave Brenda's arm a squeeze. "Let's tell Janey to pack. I'll call Peter, and we'll get on the road this morning."

Brenda hugged her tightly. "Thank you. Thank you."

Mallory drew back. "But I want to hear from you at least twice a day."

Brenda grinned. "Yes, Mother."

This was the best way to handle this, Brenda reminded herself when more second thoughts attempted to intrude. She could focus on finding answers and Janey would be safely away from the trouble.

Ben appeared at the door, all smiles with a tiara on his head.

Now, if she could really trust this man…she might just get through this.

Chapter Seven

11:50 a.m.

From her front door Brenda waved again as Mallory drove away.

Her chest felt so tight she could barely breathe. She hoped this had been the right decision. Having Mallory take her child a four-hour drive away was terrifying. No matter that she trusted the woman implicitly. Brenda had spent two nights in Los Angeles with Janey here under the nanny's careful watch. Why worry about a fraction of that distance now?

Because everything was different now. Vastly more uncertain and no little bit terrifying.

Brenda wasn't sure who or what to trust. She stared at the man standing on the sidewalk that led from his house to the street. He paced back and forth, his cell phone pressed to his ear. Could she trust him? Was the mere idea a mistake?

He'd given every indication that she could…but so had Scott. She'd been married to him for six years and hadn't realized what he was capable of beyond the cheating until only yesterday.

She had never considered herself a fool. But she had definitely been fooled by Scott. A repeat of that mistake was not something she wanted to make—ever.

Despite understanding this reality, she also recognized that she needed help.

She could not do this alone. At least, it wouldn't be smart to attempt an investigation of her own without help. This was serious…dangerous.

Frankly, she wasn't entirely sure where to start. At this point, Detective Shelton was being overly secretive. He'd asked her plenty of questions about Scott and his business this morning, but he'd sidestepped her every attempt at questions of her own. Like what would Scott be doing in Los Angeles? Was he hiding there? Shelton couldn't answer the question. Or wouldn't, was more like it.

No matter that she and Janey were victims in this bizarre situation, she had a feeling Shelton saw her as a potential suspect. Which was ridiculous. Yes, she had lived with Scott for five years. Yes, they had a child together. But obviously that didn't mean he shared every detail of his business life with her or that he told her the whole truth with anything he did share. In all honesty, she had no idea if anything she knew about her husband was real, much less true.

Who hadn't seen situations like this in the movies? A wife who discovered all manner of bad things about a suddenly missing husband. The wife always ended up facing conflict. And the horrifying realities always came as a surprise.

Brenda rolled her eyes. She was a writer, for heaven's sake. She made her living coming up with scenarios not unlike this one and still she hadn't seen it coming. No doubt her career made her look all the more suspicious to the authorities. Shelton hadn't said as much yet but that didn't mean he wasn't already considering the possibility. Sadly, it happened. Wives killed husbands…husbands killed wives.

Not only did she need to find whatever trouble Scott had

gotten himself into, she needed to protect herself and Janey. That was the bottom line of her current reality.

Ben's call ended and he headed her way. At the same time a dark four-door sedan eased to the curb in front of her house. The urge to stamp her foot and demand "What now?" proved nearly overwhelming.

The driver's-side door opened, and a figure emerged from the car. Dark suit jacket…dark hair.

The FBI agent.

What was his name?

Cummings. Special Agent Jarrod Cummings.

She was supposed to call him about an appointment today. Apparently he had grown impatient and decided to just show up. Or maybe Shelton had given him a heads-up about the latest developments in the Devers saga.

Perfect. Just what she needed. She suddenly felt utterly weary.

Ben was already halfway up her sidewalk by the time the agent opened her gate.

As Ben stepped up onto her porch, he asked her, "The FBI agent, right?"

She nodded. "He was supposed to wait for my call."

Ben glanced at her. "They can be pushy sometimes."

Just her luck.

As he had yesterday, Agent Cummings wore a dark suit that looked slightly rumpled. He was clean-shaven this time, though his hair looked a little tousled. Weren't federal agents supposed to be known for their pristine attire and presentation? Evidently not this one.

"Ms. Devers," the agent said as he approached her steps. He glanced at Ben and gave him a subtle nod.

"I planned to call you," Brenda explained, "but we've had a rough night around here, so I haven't gotten around to it."

"The break-in," he said as he stepped up first one, then the next step.

So he had heard. Shelton must want to be rid of this case if he was in such a hurry to pass along the latest updates to a federal agent.

"Yes. It was quite an ordeal."

He glanced at Ben once more before settling his gaze back on her. "If you're available now, I would like to get started with our interview."

Why put it off? "Sure. We can talk now."

The agent's gaze settled on Ben yet again. "The neighbor," he said. "Ben, isn't it?"

Ben thrust out his hand. "Ben Clark."

Cummings shook the extended hand. Brenda didn't bother to ask how he knew Ben's name or that he was her neighbor.

Before the agent could suggest otherwise, Brenda announced, "I would like Ben to sit in on the interview."

"Are you an attorney, Mr. Clark?" Cummings asked.

Ben smiled. "No. Just a friend."

"Do you know Mr. Devers?" the man prodded.

"No," Brenda interjected. The question infuriated her because she understood what the agent was getting at. "Ben is new to the neighborhood. Scott was already dead—missing—when he moved in next door."

Cummings bobbed his head in a noncommittal nod that blatantly declared he didn't believe her. "Very well, shall we get started?"

Brenda turned her back on him and walked into her house. Cummings came in behind her and Ben right after him. She settled on the sofa and let the two men sit where they would. She was too tired and too angry to summon any manners.

"Your husband," Cummings began.

"He stopped being my husband nearly a year ago," Brenda countered, setting the record straight. "He just hadn't signed the divorce papers yet." She was sick to death of everyone calling Scott her husband. He'd stopped being her husband when he cheated for the third time—that she knew of.

"Scott," Cummings amended with a look that suggested what she'd said ticked some box in his brain.

Brenda struggled to tamp down her fury. She did not want to end up making herself look more suspicious. He was probably already putting two and two together and coming up with Ben as Brenda's new lover.

She was so sick of this.

"The point Brenda is making," Ben said during the ensuing silence, "is that Scott had stopped sharing details of his life, business or personal, with her one year ago. Perhaps even before that. She is only aware of what he allowed her to know. He was clearly keeping secrets well before their separation."

Cummings eyed him speculatively. "And you know all this how?"

Ben smiled patiently. "Last evening—over pizza as you'll recall—Brenda shared her concerns about Scott's behavior over the past year or so. I'm certain if you interview Mallory Lawrence, the nanny employed by Brenda for the past two-plus years, you can confirm as much."

Brenda was pleasantly surprised at her neighbor's ability to summarize the situation so accurately and concisely.

Cummings nodded then turned back to her. "Your—Scott Devers was deeply involved with money laundering. A South American branch of the Jalisco cartel, with whom he and his partner were doing business, is most unhappy with this recent turn of events."

He'd lost her at money laundering. No matter that she and Ben had discussed the possibility, to have it confirmed by this FBI agent was unnerving. Obviously she had known given the events of the past couple of days that whatever Scott had done was bad…but she hadn't wanted to believe it would be this bad. On a scale of one to ten this was a clear twelve.

"Has the Bureau," Ben asked, "confirmed these accusations or are you speculating?"

Excellent question. Brenda was so grateful to have an objective view of the situation on her side.

Cummings swung his attention to the man seated on the sofa with Brenda. "The Bureau has been watching Scott Devers and Tate Jenner for fifteen months. We have documented their criminal behavior all this time."

Brenda felt sick to her stomach. But then her anger stirred. These people had allowed her and her daughter to live here in this house—in this town—like sitting ducks while they orchestrated an investigation that involved a South American cartel. What the hell?

Before she could demand to know why she and Janey hadn't been protected or at least warned, Ben spoke once more. "Then you're aware that Brenda is not involved with the firm. She has no knowledge of the clients or the activities of the firm. And certainly she has no information about any cartel dealings."

"That may be," Cummings admitted, "but there's just one problem."

Brenda held her breath. She couldn't imagine what was coming next.

"Ten months ago Scott Devers agreed to be an informant

for the Bureau. He made a claim that if anything happened to him there was an insurance policy to back up all that he had shared with us. Obviously, based on the message left on your garage door last night—" he directed this to Brenda "—someone else is aware of his backup plan."

"Insurance policy?" Brenda repeated. "What does that mean?" She had an idea. The creative side of her brain was spinning wildly. A list, she presumed. Details of accounts or money transfers. Something that would be a problem for the cartel.

Cummings turned up his hands. "No idea. He never expounded on the comment."

"Then he didn't make this comment to you," Ben suggested, or maybe it was more than a suggestion. The way he was staring down the agent it was as if he knew exactly what Cummings meant.

"He did not."

"His handler," Ben said. "He has a handler and this is who he told."

"Had," Cummings corrected. "The third victim, Special Agent Clinton Pratt, was his handler."

Brenda's jaw dropped. She didn't need to ask… She didn't even need to hear more. Wherever Scott was—if he wasn't dead—he was in the crosshairs of more than just the cartel. The FBI wanted him in all probability just as badly. As if she'd said her thoughts aloud, Cummings turned his attention to Brenda. No matter that she was certain she didn't want to hear whatever was coming next… She'd already heard enough for a dozen lifetimes.

"Do yourself a favor, Ms. Devers," the agent said. "Make sure you really know who your friends—" he glanced at Ben "—and your neighbors are before you trust them. I think the hole you've dug for yourself and your daughter—whether by design or out of obliviousness—is already deep enough. Don't keep digging."

With that he rose from his chair. "You have my card. Call me when you're ready to talk further." Then he walked out.

Chapter Eight

12:45 p.m.

Ben hadn't expected to have to explain himself under these circumstances. But the way Brenda was looking at him, he had no choice. It was time to come clean or risk losing her trust entirely. She had been lied to so much, even the slightest hint of skirting the truth was an egregious offence.

"Agent Cummings has an agenda—find the facts at any cost. Today that cost was an attempt at unsettling you," Ben started to explain, but she cut him off.

"No," she argued. "He was trying to warn me. Why would he do that?"

"I'll tell you everything," he assured her. "I have no reason to keep anything from you…now."

"Now?" She stood, took a step away from the sofa and him, arms folded protectively over her chest. "I want to know everything now." Fury tightened the features of her face. "Right now."

She was worried and she had every right to be. This business her—Scott had allowed himself to fall into was deadly. As much as Ben wanted to stand and reach out to her, he knew better. So, he remained seated. Whatever necessary to make her feel comfortable and hopefully safe in his presence.

"My name is Ben Clark, and I'm from Illinois." He studied her expression as he spoke. Hoping to see something besides the anger and disappointment. "I grew up on a farm, just as I told you, and the focus of my work is people—sometimes observing them, other times working with them to sort out a situation. Sometimes protecting them. I am employed by the Colby Agency, a private investigations firm in Chicago. I assure you I am not here to cause trouble or to harm you or your daughter in any way. I'm here to help."

Her eyes narrowed to suspicious slits. "If you work for a private investigations firm then someone hired you. It wasn't me. Who was it?"

"Would you sit down with me, please?" He didn't want to answer her with her standing there looking ready to run… or to crumble.

She sidestepped to the chair vacated by the agent who'd offhandedly outed him. When she'd eased down onto the cushion, he braced his forearms on his knees and allowed his hands to hang, unmoving in clear view. He needed her calm and rational. With her and her child's safety hanging in the balance, he recognized that it was difficult for her to be either one.

"Tell me," she demanded, "who hired you? The cartel? Lena Jenner?" Outrage had chased away some of her uncertainty and propped up her bravado. "Oh my God, it was Lena, wasn't it? She's trying to make sure she and her family are in the clear." She shook her head. "I can't believe this. She and I have known each other for years. How could she do this? How could she believe I would be involved in this in any way?"

"Ms. Jenner did not hire me," he said. "I've never met her or spoken with her."

"Well, then who? Obviously it wasn't the other victim. The..." She shook her head in frustration. "The FBI handler, Pratt. Who does that leave?" Her face paled. "The cartel hired you. Oh my God." She shot to her feet once more.

He stood then, held up his hands surrender-style.

"Brenda," he said, wishing she would just sit back down and take a moment, "your *husband* hired me."

Her breath caught, the sound tearing at him. He hadn't wanted this moment to happen this way. "I don't believe you," she argued.

The shine of emotion in her eyes tightened his chest. Brenda was a good person. She didn't deserve what was happening to her and her daughter, but it was done. The only thing Ben could do at this point was attempt to protect her from what was transpiring and what without doubt was coming next.

"It's difficult to believe," he admitted. "But if you'll hear me out, I think you'll understand."

One shoulder moved up and then fell as if she couldn't care less. "Keep talking."

"Two months ago, Scott recognized he was in over his head. He set up a secret meeting with my employer and presented his case. According to him, his partner, Tate Jenner, had lured him into a deal with the devil—those were his words."

Brenda shook her head. "Of course, he would blame someone else. Scott never took responsibility for his own actions."

Ben acknowledged her conclusion with a nod. He'd gathered as much about Scott Devers over the past few weeks. "From what we've been able to ascertain, he was likely telling the truth in this instance. Jenner appeared to have made the first move with the Jalisco cartel. Since their firm, J&D Investments, was failing, it was only a matter of time before they lost everything. The last couple of years were difficult on everyone. The smaller firms like theirs have repeatedly been the first to fall."

She sucked in a breath, then moistened her lips. "Okay, let's say you're right so far. I'm still not convinced he did this for me or for Janey. But I'm prepared to keep listening."

That was all he could ask for.

"Tate convinced Scott they never had to get their hands dirty," Ben went on. "Just take the cartel's money and invest it. Return the proceeds, keeping a share for their trouble. It was a win-win situation, and no one was going to be hurt by it. To his way of thinking they weren't selling drugs or trafficking people…they were simply serving as a bank. Banks set up accounts for bad people all the time. If they didn't do it, someone else would. This was how Jenner justified what they were doing. Eventually Scott bought into it."

"Except banks," she argued, "don't recognize the serial killers and criminals from the other people who walk through their doors wanting to set up an account. Scott and Tate knew these were bad people when they agreed to take them on." She squeezed her eyes shut and shook her head.

"I'm not justifying the decision," Ben said, in hopes of somehow regaining her confidence despite the sticky situation. "But the decision he made to come to the Colby Agency was a good one. It was a good choice made by a man who, despite his past bad choices, cared about his family."

She laughed out loud then. "Please. I've told you all about him. How can you say anything even remotely nice about him?"

He got it. He really did. "I'm not saying he was a good

husband, Brenda. I'm saying when the chips were down, he did the right thing as a human."

"Like being in the Los Angeles area with some blonde and pretending he didn't see me." She sent Ben a look that said *top that one.*

"The agency has confirmed that Scott did board a plane in Los Angeles. His destination was Nashville, about two hours or so north of here."

She stared at him a moment. "How did you confirm this? Surely Scott didn't use his name. I've never known him to be that kind of careless about himself. He wouldn't have wanted to take the risk."

"He used the name Stan Dayton. We have a contact who confirmed his ID via the airport's facial recognition system. I'm sure Agent Cummings and Detective Shelton are aware of this already but are not prepared to share it with you."

"I can't believe this." She held up her hands in obvious frustration. "Anyway, you've convinced me that he retained the services of your agency. Explain to me what that entails."

"Scott asked that if anything happened to him or he disappeared, that we were to step in and protect his family until the situation was resolved. He leased the house next door when the previous owner moved. He suspected there was going to be trouble. My assignment is to keep an eye on you and Janey. Protect you from physical harm if the need arises and help you navigate the fallout from this investigation."

"Then how did that intruder get into my house if you're supposed to be watching? Why didn't you stop him?" she demanded.

"I intercepted him," he explained, "in the alley." He gingerly touched the back of his head. "But he had a friend. The blow came from behind me. When I came to, the police were already here. Believe me, no one is more frustrated and disappointed about that than me."

The horrified expression on her face told him she wasn't sure whether to be angry or worried. "Are you all right?"

"Other than a lingering headache, I'm okay."

"Do you need medical attention?" Her face had softened now.

"No. Really, I'm fine. The only thing I need is for you to understand who I am and why I'm here." He smiled hopefully. "And maybe to trust me."

Brenda appeared to consider all he'd said for a bit before she spoke again. "So, I'm supposed to believe that you're here to protect me." She shook her head, her expression weary. "I'm sorry, Ben, you seem like a nice guy, but I need something more concrete than your word. This is my daughter's life—my life—we're talking about here."

"Fair enough. The Colby Agency is among the top, most prestigious investigative agencies in the country. Whatever else your husband is guilty of, he made an excellent choice by coming to us. Let me make a call. I want to introduce you to the woman in charge. I think when you hear what she has to say, you'll understand."

Ben reached for his cell phone and put through a call to Victoria's direct line. She answered immediately. "Victoria, I'm here with Brenda Devers. We need to have that face to face."

"Give me one minute," Victoria said. "I'll set up a video call."

The call ended.

"She'll call right back, using video," he explained. "Meanwhile, feel free to search the Colby Agency on the web. You'll find images of Victoria and Jamie. They run the agency. You'll see the reviews. Read them. Then you'll understand."

Whether Brenda realized it or not, she could not be in better hands.

Chapter Nine

1:00 p.m.

Still reeling with emotions, Brenda reached for her phone and did as Ben suggested. She opened a browser, typed in the Colby Agency of Chicago and hit Search.

Line after line of relevant information filled the screen.

Former clients lauded the agency, the staff and the results of their work. Thousands of reviews were available. She scanned the photos of Victoria and Jamie. Theirs were the only images available of staff members. She supposed investigators like Ben weren't shown for the protection of ongoing cases.

No matter how Brenda framed her search criteria, the conclusions were the same: The Colby Agency was the very best. No complaints…no outstanding issues. Only thankful clients and glowing recommendations.

The sound of an incoming call made her jump. She looked to Ben, who'd tapped the screen of his phone. His employer was apparently returning his call. Brenda squared her shoulders and braced for this next step in her ongoing nightmare.

Scott had hired a private investigator to help her and Janey if anything happened to him…but had anything really happened to him? He was alive… She'd seen him.

It was nearly too much. She felt like coiling into a ball to hide until this whole thing was over. But real life didn't work that way. She had no choice but to face whatever the hell he had gotten them into. It was difficult to be grateful for any steps he'd taken under the circumstances. Why wasn't he here trying to protect them himself?

Right now, more than anything, she wished she could get her hands on him. The idea that he would hide while they dealt with this mess infuriated her. The least he could do was turn himself in to the FBI—the people he had agreed to work with. Why the hell was he hiding from them?

From her?

Because he was a self-centered ass!

"Victoria, Jamie," Ben said, "this is Brenda Devers."

Brenda lifted her gaze to the screen and the two women there. She wasn't sure what to say. With effort she forced a shaky smile. "Good afternoon." Though it was far from good, actually.

"Brenda," Victoria, the older of the two, said, "this is a difficult time for you. You can rest assured that Ben is one of our top investigators. He will do whatever is necessary to protect you and your daughter while navigating the puzzle this situation has put in front of you."

"We're doing all in our power," Jamie chimed in, "to track Scott's movements since the explosion. We have little to report at this time, but we will be keeping Ben apprised of our findings."

Brenda nodded, uncertain how to respond. Once more she found herself in a situation that felt utterly surreal.

"When Scott retained our services," Victoria went on, "our goal was to familiarize ourselves with him and those close to him—specifically you and Janey—in preparation for whatever steps we would need to take if and when the worst happened. But now that Scott is unaccounted for, our primary goal is to keep the two of you safe. All else is secondary."

Brenda couldn't argue with the way Victoria and Jamie laid out the agency's plan and, based on what she had read in those reviews, there was every reason to trust their motives as presented.

She looked at Ben, then back to the faces on the screen. "My daughter is with a friend at her family cabin. For now, I believe she's safe."

"We've found no reason to believe otherwise," Jamie agreed. "Although, we are still verifying background details on Mallory. To date she appears to be exactly who she represents herself as being. Her parents check out. That said, we won't stop looking until we feel completely confident we haven't missed anything. We're doing the same with your closest neighbors and anyone involved with the investment firm."

"Mallory has been Janey's nanny for two years," Brenda reminded Jamie. "I have no reason not to trust her."

"Still," Jamie returned, "we'll keep digging just in case—as we will with all the others connected in any way with your family."

"I appreciate your efforts." She really did. Maybe more than she'd realized. There were so many possibilities and details she didn't know; she was genuinely grateful for the support of such a prestigious agency. "With all that's happened, what should I do next?"

The idea of sitting around here waiting for the next shoe to drop didn't feel right.

"We searched the house and garage," Ben spoke up then, "before the intruder. Huntsville PD has done the same. I say we look again just to be sure nothing was missed. This time we'll focus on any potential hiding places Scott may have created specifically for concealing this insurance policy he claimed to have."

Though Brenda couldn't imagine where that hiding place could be, she was game. "Whatever we have to do. I would really like to find some answers so perhaps my daughter can come home." She missed her desperately already.

"At this time, I believe that's the best plan," Victoria agreed. "We will keep you informed of anything new we discover. We are here to help in whatever way you need, Brenda."

"Thank you." Brenda swallowed at the lump stuck in her throat. She'd never expected to find herself in a situation like this one. No matter how many mystery or suspense stories she had created, she had never once envisioned being thrust into the middle of a real-life one.

Ben ended the call and turned to her. "At the risk of sounding repetitive, I know this is a troubling time, but I hope you recognize now that I'm here to help."

She nodded. She was convinced and relieved. If this man had misled her the way Scott had so many times, Brenda wasn't sure she would have ever been able to trust another man ever. That her instincts had been right about him was reassuring. "I do and, as I told your employer, I am grateful for your support."

"We can start our second round of searching in the garage," he suggested, "and we can put things in order as we go along. That's only a small thing, but it may help you feel as if we're getting your life back in order on some level."

"That would be great." The mess the intruder and then the police had left felt somehow reflective of the state of her world. She couldn't fix the issues that had intruded into her life, but she could straighten up the disarray around her to the degree possible. If she were lucky, she would find something useful to solve this unsettling mystery as well.

Some would say recent events were great story fodder, but Brenda wasn't sure her readers would ever believe anyone—particularly a heroine in one of her stories—would be so naive as to have missed what her husband was up to for all that time.

No going there.

At the back door, Brenda grabbed her car fob from her handbag. Continuing to dwell on the reasons for all that was happening wouldn't solve anything. It was a waste of time to punish herself for not realizing what Scott was up to the past couple of years. Particularly since they had been separated for an entire twelve months. She rarely had any idea what he was doing. He typically let her know when he would be out of town or if for some reason he couldn't have his visit with Janey at the agreed-upon time, but that was about it.

He certainly hadn't warned her that he would be in the Los Angeles area because she had thought he was dead! She still couldn't figure out how they had both ended up there at the same time. Her meeting was set by her agent, so she'd had nothing to do with the timing. Had Scott known somehow? Chosen a flight around the same time as hers just to rattle her? To send a message? Or maybe to warn her about the coming DNA results. He surely recognized that would be coming.

And once she was officially made aware that he hadn't died in the explosion, the least he could have done was let his daughter know he was alive. What kind of person hurt the people he supposedly cared about this way? This was not some missed weekend visit… This was… She couldn't think about it anymore.

She glanced at the man walking into the garage with her.

At least Scott appeared to have done one thing right. He'd ensured they had someone to help them through this mess. She had to give him that.

If she had the chance when this was over, she intended to let him have it. Even if he somehow managed to come out of this without serving prison time, she would never allow him unsupervised visitation with Janey. Never. Nor would she ever trust him on any level.

In the garage, the mess looked worse now than before. Brenda grimaced. At least Ben had painted over the message left on the overhead door. The question—*WHERE IS IT?*—hung over her like a dark cloud. She was grateful not to have to stare at it.

"I'll back my car out," she offered. "Then I'll start with the decorations." Colorful ornaments were scattered over the floor like a pinball machine had exploded.

Ben gave a nod. "I can start with the tree. Check the inside of the pole sections that hold the limbs."

Brenda would not have thought of looking there. "Good idea."

She backed her car into the alley, careful to park to one side so as not to block the passage of others. There was really no traffic, but the three residents whose garages backed up to the alley used it regularly.

Maybe if she were writing the situation into a scene in one of her books she might have a better perspective—that omniscient view. But with this being so real and so personal it wasn't as easy as creating fiction. She almost laughed; this was certainly a perfect example of the adage "stranger than fiction."

Back in the garage, she closed the overhead door and began the frustrating process. She turned a plastic container upright and started to repack the scattered items. Thankfully most of her ornaments were plastic so they hadn't shattered. She carefully smoothed out the crumpled packing paper to ensure nothing had been written on any of it or was tucked into the folds and wrinkles. As she went through the motions, her mind sharpened to the possibilities. She checked beneath the containers. Inside even the smallest box and package. All the little things Janey had made—yarn angels, craft paper pumpkins, so many little things—made Brenda smile. Made her heart lighter.

Once Christmas and Easter as well as Halloween decor was packed away, she started on the treasures she had saved from her parents' home. Most of the pieces were inside her home. But there were some things she really hadn't been able to use but hadn't wanted to part with. Those she carefully repacked, inspecting each one methodically first.

It took nearly an hour to get the job done, but when she dusted her hands, the garage was back in order, and she felt a new sense of buoyancy.

"That wasn't so bad," Ben suggested with a smile.

"Not if you say it quickly enough." She laughed, the sound weary. "I am a little disappointed that we didn't find anything." She took a long look around. "But at least it's back in order. I'm very grateful for that."

"Believe it or not," he pointed out, "investigators spend most of their time doing exactly this—turning over rocks and finding nothing relevant to the case."

"Good to know it's not just us." She smiled, a real one, couldn't help herself. She had needed a hint of humor after the last twenty-four hours. It was one thing to be surprised by a sudden death or other disturbing life event, but then to have the situation twisted around and turned upside down and then tossed back at her was a whole other level of misery.

He hitched a thumb toward the alley where she'd parked her car. "I can pull it back in now, if you'd like."

"Sure. Thanks." She slipped the fob from her back pocket and tossed it to him.

He caught it and headed out to the alley.

The chirp of the fob sounded. A split second later an explosion echoed in the air.

Ben was suddenly rushing toward her…and then they were on the concrete floor of the garage.

Maybe it was the shock of the explosion, or the way Ben wrapped himself around her and rolled, but she hadn't felt the impact of landing. For a moment some imperceptible sound hummed in her ears, blocking out all else.

Her gaze locked with his. "What the hell was that?" she asked, or maybe she yelled.

She couldn't be sure…couldn't breathe…then she realized it was the weight of his body atop her own. As if he'd sensed this, he got up, pulled her with him. He ushered her toward the walk-through door.

"Stay here while I have a look."

Brenda didn't argue. Her head was still spinning. She watched him walk away. Blinked once, twice before her gaze rested on her car. The driver's-side door was missing…

She frowned, then noticed the damaged door lying on the apron leading up from the driveway into the garage at the open overhead door. Part of the driver's seat was twisted and blackened. What the hell…? She stared again, tried to piece together what she was seeing. Her car door had been torn off…

Ben disappeared from view then returned to her garage.

"The alley is clear. No one was injured and there appears to be no other damage to your or other property. Just the car."

It was then that she realized what he was saying. Her car had been damaged by an explosion—a bomb. The damage was limited only to her car. No one else was in the alley so no injuries.

Someone had put a bomb in her car.

Her knees buckled.

His hand caught her by the arm before she crumpled. He pulled her close. "Everything is all right. I'll call Detective Shelton."

But it wasn't all right.

That bomb hadn't been about scaring her or sending a message.

Someone had tried to kill her.

3:20 p.m.

BEN SPLIT HIS attention between the bevy of uniformed personnel in the alley and the garage where Brenda waited. She had asked to go into the house, but he didn't want her out of his sight. And one of them had to talk to Shelton.

At this point, it was fairly clear that the small bomb had been placed just beneath the driver's-side door. The device had been activated by the short-range radio transmitter in the key fob. The only reason it hadn't been activated when Brenda moved the car was because the door had been unlocked, so there had been no reason for the transmission. She hadn't locked the vehicle when she parked in the alley, but Ben hadn't known this. Most vehicles locked automatically after a few minutes once the driver walked away with the fob. But Brenda had turned off that option to ensure her daughter could get out if for any reason she was ever left in the car.

When Ben went to move the car he had hit the unlock button on the fob out of habit.

Thank God he had.

Shelton's people insisted they had checked her car when they went over the garage, which, assuming they had been thorough in their search, meant the bomb had been added at some point since that time. Neither he nor Brenda had used her car since her return from Los Angeles, so that was possible.

The device wasn't a complex one. Based on what was left of the small case, a magnet had held it to the bottom of the vehicle. There would hopefully be more information available once the lab had finished its work.

Ben wasn't particularly surprised by the act. Cartels often sent enforcers or *sicarios*—hit men—to do their dirty work. To scare with threatening messages, to injure or kill. It wasn't unusual, but what this level of enforcement suggested was the significance of the item or items they were looking for. Clearly the cartel had deemed the loss particularly important, and they were growing impatient for its return.

This was something he would very much have liked to know before the explosion, but he knew now. Thankfully no one had been hurt.

When Detective Shelton started for the garage, Ben joined him. Brenda watched the two of them approach, dread evident in her posture. It was difficult to be left with the fallout when you had no idea what it related to.

"We're taking your car in," Shelton advised Brenda. "I think it's pointless to take prints from the garage again, but we will go over the car thoroughly. If we find anything we'll let you know."

Brenda nodded her understanding. "Should I call my insurance company?"

She had chosen not to call about the intruder since nothing had appeared to be missing and none of the windows or doors in her home were damaged by the invasion.

"Yes," Shelton replied. "Although I can't give you a firm release date, it's best to advise them of the situation and go with whatever they suggest."

Brenda hugged herself. "They'll probably cancel on me. I think it's the same insurance company as Scott used for the firm."

It happened. Like any other business, insurance companies had a degree of risk they were willing to assume and anything beyond that point was unacceptable. Ben hoped for her sake it didn't become an issue. She was dealing with enough already.

Shelton pointed to the cleared garage floor with the pen in his hand. "You put everything away."

"I needed to be doing something." Brenda drew in a big breath. "This escalating situation has me on edge, and I can't just sit around waiting to hear from you."

"It's not easy, I'm sure." The detective's brow furrowed. "Did you find anything that might have some bearing on the case?"

"I would have called you about it if I had," Brenda tossed back. "I'm aware of my legal obligations, Detective. No one wants this resolved more than I do."

Ben bit back a grin. "If," he said to the detective, "you don't need us for anything else, we'll go inside where Ms. Devers can feel safer."

Shelton hitched his head back in acknowledgment. "If I have any further questions I'll knock on your door."

"Is it all right," Ben ventured, "if we close up and lock the garage, or do you still need access?"

"Sure. Sure." Shelton glanced around. "We don't need to be in here for anything else."

"Thank you," Brenda said. "I do appreciate all you're doing to find the person or persons responsible for…" She shook her head. "I don't even know what to call it."

"It's a difficult situation," the older man agreed. "When these things happen to the family of a criminal suspect, it's never easy or pretty."

Brenda's arms visibly tightened around her. "I can see that."

"As I said, I'll call if we find anything." Shelton turned and walked out of the garage.

Ben hit the button next to the walk-through door, closing the overhead one. While it lowered, he checked the garage's one window, ensuring it was secure.

"We can start on the house now, if you'd like." He returned to the door where Brenda waited.

"Okay." She walked out into the small backyard of her home, rubbed at her crossed arms as if she were cold. "I could make sandwiches or call for something to be delivered."

"Whatever you decide works for me." He locked the door they had exited. "I'll have another look around outside before coming in."

They had done this already, but like the garage and house, a second look never hurt. Obviously, it could save a life.

"Sure." She faked a smile and then headed into the house.

Ben called Victoria and provided an update.

"This is most unsettling," Victoria agreed. "It's the things you don't see coming that pose the highest risk."

Ben considered what he wanted to say next. His gaze lingered on the kitchen window in hopes of getting a glimpse of Brenda. This situation was bent in a direction that felt wrong to him. Off somehow. He simply hadn't figured out what that oddity was. But it was there…waiting for him to grab hold of it.

"I'm not convinced the threats so far have been as deadly as I would expect from the cartel." He was familiar with the history of the one with whom Devers had gotten involved. They weren't known for going soft on a target—even an innocent target. "There's either something else going on here or they have an ace in the hole we don't know about yet."

"We'll keep pressing forward with our research on this end," Victoria assured him. "Stay sharp, Ben. Like you, I'm concerned this is just the prelude to something far more dangerous."

Ben ended the call and started his search of the small plot of grass and shrubs around the Devers home. He wasn't sure he would find anything, but he could use the time to get his thoughts straight. This was something else he had started to recognize.

Most assigned to monitor the activities of another would confess to a growing bond—even if only forming on the part of the observer. But that bond he felt with Brenda was growing far too quickly for comfort.

It was a fine and dangerous line playing the part of protector.

Dangerous for her safety, without doubt, and dangerous to him in ways he hadn't expected.

Chapter Ten

4:30 p.m.

Brenda had called Janey. It had taken every ounce of strength she possessed not to collapse into tears just listening to her daughter's sweet voice. She hadn't been able to tell her anything about what happened, but she had spoken to Mallory afterward and explained the horrifying events to her. Brenda was so very grateful that Janey was away from this nightmare. She wasn't sure her heart could take having her daughter caught in the middle of this.

The idea that Scott didn't seem to care infuriated her. If he cared, he would be here helping to set this business to rights.

Focus on the task at hand.

She had gone through her bathroom already. Now she considered her bedroom—the one she had once shared with Scott. If he were going to hide something in her home, the home they had once shared, where would he put it?

She gazed up at the ceiling. The light fixture was the fan type with blades and lights surrounding the decorative metal housing that held the motor. Ben had checked the blades, top and bottom, as well as the exterior of the body, just as the police had. Taking the metal base apart might be necessary if they found nothing anywhere else in the house. Then again, the idea probably wasn't even reasonable since Scott hadn't been particularly handy with repairing or installing items around the house. He always called someone. She couldn't see him disassembling a ceiling fan and reinstalling it just to hide something.

She doubted he would have a clue where or how to begin.

Moving on, she once again checked behind every piece of furniture. Inside drawers as well as beneath the bottoms. She picked through socks and underthings and the array of items in each drawer. In the pockets of jackets and slacks that hung in her closet. Underneath the mattress and the bed linens. Inside the pillow covers. She checked behind hanging photos. Inside the framed ones lining the top of her dresser.

There just was nothing to find.

Frustration twisted through her. What the hell had Scott been thinking to take something from the cartel and believe he could get away with it? Had he taken whatever they wanted back for the FBI? She found it strange that Agent Cummings hadn't shown up after the door was blown off her car—the driver's-side door.

She could have been killed.

Before she could stop the memories, she had flashes of Ben wrapping his arms around her and protecting her from the fall to the unforgiving concrete floor. She shivered as much from the remembered feel of his arms around her as from the shock of the explosion. He had protected her… putting himself in the path of any potential flying debris. He had helped her through the moments that followed while she struggled to come to terms with the new level of her nightmare.

"Any luck in here?"

She jumped. Whipped around to face the door, hand on her chest.

"Sorry." Ben held up his hands. "I didn't mean to startle you. I've finished up in the living room and kitchen area."

Brenda steadied herself. Wow, he worked fast. But then, this house wasn't filled with memories for him. Those memories distracted her, filled her with emotions she couldn't quite sort just now.

Okay, she shook off the thought. He'd been through the main areas already. That left only the hall bath, the guest room and Janey's. "Nothing here." She drew in a deep steadying breath. "I was about to start in Janey's room."

He gave a nod. "I'll take the bathroom and your office if you have no objections."

"Sounds good."

He disappeared from the door while she lingered in the middle of her room. How many times had she said the words *sounds good* the past couple of days? When the truth was, none of this sounded good. Nothing that had happened in the past forty-eight hours was good.

Move on, Brenda. Steeling herself, she walked out of her room.

In the hall, Ben was busy checking behind the framed photographs she had hung so liberally along the walls. She liked passing the images of Janey from birth until now. Each morning as she walked from her bedroom to the kitchen she smiled at all those captured moments. She didn't mind the extra dusting. She was glad he'd thought to look there as well.

She made her way to Janey's room, and for a long moment she just stood there taking in the sight of her little girl's space. Her dolls and toys were scattered after the search by the police, but seeing the disorder reminded her of a long afternoon with Janey enjoying her toys. Why give a child dolls and other things if you weren't going to allow them to play with them? It was often messy, but it was the best kind of messiness. Scott never approved, but he didn't have the final say.

Brenda got to work. The dolls were first. She checked each one, though there were not many good places to hide anything on or in a Barbie. Once all the dolls were put away, she fixed her attention on the little wood kitchen set and all the goodies that went with it. Nothing unexpected. Then she checked the slew of stuffed animals. No holes or tears or repaired places where something may have been inserted. Nothing on, inside or behind any of her daughter's furniture.

A last look through the closet and she turned to leave the room, her heart aching at the idea that it could be days yet before she held her daughter in her arms again. She missed her so.

Her gaze snagged on the Barbie Dreamhouse. Had she checked it well enough? She had moved all the furniture, looked it over carefully before putting it back. The police had turned it over and looked beneath it.

Before her mind was even made up, she was already moving toward the big pink plastic house. She started with the slide, removing it from the house first. Piece by piece she removed each part behind or under which there could potentially be something hidden. The elevator on the opposite side from the slide was last.

Brenda eased from her knees to her bottom to sit on the hardwood. The elevator was partially loose, tilted just a bit. Came off easier than she'd expected. When she turned it over her breath caught. An address had been written on the back side where it connected to the house, rendering the words and numbers completely hidden before she pulled it free.

Bradley Street. She wasn't familiar with the location, but she thought it might be in the Merrimack Mill Village. A quick check of the map on her cell phone gave her the exact locale. She had been right. The old Merrimack Mill Village was a local historic district. She had been to the area.

Moving with new purpose, Brenda snapped a pic and then quickly put the pieces of the house back together. Janey would be horrified if she came home and found it partially disassembled. Once all was as it should be, Brenda got to her feet. Ben was no longer in the hall, her office or bathroom. She found him in the kitchen speaking quietly to someone on his phone.

She could barely restrain herself. They needed to go to this address. Maybe someone there could provide an answer or at least point them in the right direction. Telling the police was likely the right thing to do, but she absolutely refused to do so until she'd checked it out herself. Maybe it was wrong, but she wasn't entirely satisfied with the way the authorities, local and federal, were handling things so far. No one except the Colby Agency had told her that Scott really had been at the Los Angeles airport. Why was that? Surely the FBI had found the same information. The only possible answer was that they were keeping information from her. As much as she disliked the idea of sounding paranoid, she was certain of it. The reason was fairly clear. To Shelton and Cummings, she was a suspect rather than a victim.

Whatever they were thinking, she couldn't dwell on the uncertainty of it. She had to do something. Brenda gathered her handbag and tucked her phone inside. By the time Ben's call ended she was ready to go. They would need to use his car since hers had been towed to the lab.

Hers had been damaged by a bomb…meant to cause her harm.

She shuddered and suddenly wondered what her neighbors were thinking. The police had been to her home repeatedly. Anyone who lived nearby had no doubt heard all manner of rumors about the explosion even if they hadn't heard the actual explosion. Thankfully there had been no school today so only the teachers and staff had been on hand and suffered through the necessary evacuation. Numerous houses on either side of hers had been temporarily evacuated as well. All those people had waited at the end of the block until her entire property was searched for additional threats. So horrifying and humiliating. Everyone around her now knew there was something strange and nefarious going on at the Devers home.

After Scott's supposed death, so many had come by offering condolences and providing casseroles and soups. She cringed at the idea of what they would think when they learned the truth.

Hopefully she wouldn't run into anyone who had questions. The reporters had been bad enough those first two weeks after the explosion at the firm. If they got a whiff of the change to Scott's status and the escalating events at her home, they would be back. She desperately hoped that didn't happen anytime soon.

"Did you find anything?"

His question startled her. Jeez. She had to stop getting lost in thought.

"Sorry again," he said with an apologetic expression.

"It's not you. It's me." She shook her head. "I keep… Anyway. I found something." She showed him the picture she had snapped with her phone. "This was on the back side of the Barbie Dreamhouse elevator."

"Bradley Street." His gaze shifted to hers. "Do you know the place?"

"I'm familiar with the area but I don't know anyone who lives there—at least I don't think I do."

She couldn't be completely certain, since there were some people she knew whose home addresses were not something she had ever learned or needed to. Most people had acquaintances—particularly with all the social media—with whom they spoke from time to time but whose personal information they didn't really know.

"We'll see what we can find out." He glanced toward the front of the house. "I don't know if you've noticed, but you have a surveillance detail. One man in a black sedan. Judging by the vehicle and the license plate I'd say it's the Bureau."

Brenda bit her lip. That could complicate things. "Is there a way to prevent him from following us or knowing that we've left?"

"We have to use my rental car so, yes, we should be able to do that." He thought for a moment. "We'll exit through the back door here and make our way via the alley to my garage. We can drive to the other end of the alley to make our getaway, and he won't ever see us."

Unless they had someone else watching the alley.

"Let's give it a try." Her nerves were jumping. She wanted to see what or who was at this address. Surely if Scott had written the address in a place no one was likely to find it then it meant something. But what?

The real question was how had he known she would find it?

No. Wait. She got it. Because this was something she did in her books. If there were hidden clues, they were always in some unsuspecting place. Oh yes. That was it. He had known she would look for exactly the sort of place he'd chosen. A place the police and anyone else searching was *not* likely to look. Not to mention she was the one who put that Barbie Dreamhouse together and she had not left any wobbly parts. The fact that the elevator was loose, askew just the tiniest bit, had ensured she would check it.

Her confidence building, she followed Ben through the back door. She locked it and hoped the man watching her house didn't notice them leaving. The trees and shrubs were fairly thick so she expected he wouldn't. Still, the possibility made her nervous. It would be dark soon but waiting until then was not happening. She needed answers and she needed to be able to see the house before approaching it.

Actually, she admitted if only to herself, she had no idea what she needed except answers.

In the alley, she followed Ben to his garage. He entered the code and the door opened with a slow groan and grind. She winced at the noise it generated. Once they were in the garage, he did a thorough search of his car—to ensure there were no devices for tracking or causing harm, he explained. Even after his careful examination, a moment was required for her to work up the nerve to get inside. Brenda wasn't sure she would ever look at approaching or climbing into a vehicle the same way.

While she buckled up, he backed out of the garage and lowered the door by pressing a button on the bottom of his rearview mirror. At the end of the alley, she held her breath as they pulled out onto Holmes Avenue. It wasn't that far to the mill village, but the hour ensured plenty of commuters.

As he navigated traffic and made the necessary turns, he kept an eye on the street behind them. Obviously he had done this many times before. Brenda followed his example, dividing her attention between the passenger-door side mirror and the street in front of them. It wasn't that she wanted to hide her movements from the authorities. Her intent was not to deceive anyone. But she needed to check things out before the police, otherwise she might not be given the full details. Though she trusted the police mostly, she recognized that there were some things they weren't allowed to tell her or chose not to because of her status as a potential suspect.

As awful as all of this was, she couldn't deny it certainly gave her a whole new perspective on how this side of an investigation felt. A good storyteller used moments like this as research. Maybe if she focused on that aspect of this nightmare, it would make getting through this easier.

"Turn there," she told Ben as he neared the intersection with Triana Boulevard.

The past few years the southwest side of Huntsville had been making a comeback. Lots of people were buying up the old millhouses and renovating. Businesses were filling the once empty warehouses and abandoned retail spaces. She'd read about the revival.

"What do you mean when you say you're familiar with the neighborhood? Have you lived in the area?"

She hauled her attention from beyond the window and turned to the driver. "No. I mean I'm familiar with the area in a very general way. Several local bookstores joined forces and held a signing event at Merrimack Hall last year." She pointed to the building as they passed it. "And I think there used to be a ceramic shop along this block that I visited once." She leaned forward to better see the street signs. "We'll take the next right, Holly Avenue."

"Do you participate in book signings often?" He glanced at her as he made the turn onto Holly.

"Sometimes. Not so much now as in past years." She stared at the street ahead. "Everything changes. Especially after you have a child." She pointed to the upcoming intersection. "That's Bradley. We're going left."

He slowed and they scanned the numbers on the mailboxes. "Looks like the next house on the left," he said as he slowed a bit more.

Brenda stared at the house. Looked vacant. Disappointment rattled through her. Then again, looks could be deceiving. Like most of the rentals in the village, the house was a duplex. No curtains or blinds on the windows on either side.

Ben parked at the curb. "I can have a look around first," he offered.

She reached for her seat belt and unfastened it. "I'd prefer to go with you."

He gave her a nod. "Let's do it then."

They emerged from the car together, met at the hood. A single sidewalk led to the porch, then split off to meet two sets of steps. The one on the right was their destination. The door was a solid wood one with no windows. While Ben knocked, Brenda wandered to the first of the two large windows along the wall next to it. She put her hands on either side of her face and peered through the grimy glass. The front room appeared empty. Her hopes sank. The place was vacant.

"The front room is empty," she said as she walked past Ben to the set of windows next to the neighboring front door.

Ben knocked once more. "What about that side?"

She peered beyond the window, then groaned. "Looks empty too."

Ben smiled.

"Why are you smiling?" A dead end. That's what this was. Irritation flickered deep inside her.

"That just means we get to go around back." He gestured toward the steps.

She smiled. "Good point." Brenda was way past beating around the bush here. She needed answers. She wanted her daughter back…her life back.

Ben checked the street before they walked around the right side of the house. The houses were old, end of the nineteenth century old. Most had been wrapped in vinyl siding and the side porches closed in to add additional floor space. This one was no different, but the addition of a rear porch provided another easily accessible view into the house. Ben climbed the rear steps first. He moved from the two smaller windows to the door.

Brenda was right behind him. Cupping her face, she stared through those windows too. Still nothing. No furniture. No leftover household goods at all. With both sides of the duplex vacant, she would have expected a For Rent sign out front.

"The door is ajar."

Brenda looked from him to the door. It was open just a crack. "If we go in…"

"Illegal entrance," he finished for her.

"I'll go in," she said, moving toward the door. "I'm not in law enforcement and I have no real reason to know the rules." Except she did. She used them in her stories all the time. She imagined that would work against her in a court of law.

"Funny," he countered. "We'll both go in. In my opinion, we were invited."

Brenda chuckled. "I love the way you think." She'd have to remember that line.

The back door entered into the kitchen. There was a musty, dank smell about the house as if it hadn't been lived in for a very long time. Some of the cabinet doors hung from a single hinge. Others were missing altogether. A few soda and beer cans were lying around on the floor. A burger wrapper and pizza box on the counter. Thankfully nothing scary like needles or other drug paraphernalia. More beer cans stood in one corner of the living room. An old blanket was on the floor under a window.

"Brenda."

She turned to him, and that was when she spotted the writing on the wall behind them—the one that separated the kitchen from the front room. The message looked exactly like the one left in black spray paint on her garage door.

YOU ARE RUNNING OUT OF TIME.

Fear spread through Brenda like frost creeping through her veins, freezing all that it touched. Then, as if her emotions had shifted into an unexpected reverse, outrage abruptly roared inside her.

How was she supposed to find something when she had no idea what she was looking for?

Chapter Eleven

Vacant Duplex
Bradley Street
Huntsville, 5:30 p.m.

Outside the house they sat in the car. The silence had thickened to the point Ben wanted to reach out to her. She hadn't spoken since reading the message on the wall. Ben didn't ask if she was okay. Of course she wasn't. Every damned thing that happened only opened up more questions. There just didn't appear to be any answers.

He had a feeling this was someone's twisted idea of a game. He had his doubts about whether the cartel would play around this way. This felt more and more like someone who got burned or shortchanged by Devers and now that person wanted to find whatever was missing. Maybe before the cartel learned of the situation.

Ben turned to his passenger. "Let's consider our timeline for a moment."

She looked to him. Blinked. He couldn't decide based on the deadpan expression on her face if she was scared, angry or numb. Maybe a little of all three.

"The intruder came into your home very early this morning. He left you that note on the garage door. Then, this afternoon, in our follow-up search, we find the address in the dollhouse."

Another slow blink and vague nod.

"My question is, how difficult was it to remove the Barbie elevator and then to put it back?" Sounded completely ridiculous but he had a point.

She considered the question for a moment. "It doesn't take long. Detaching it makes a couple of snapping noises, as does pushing it into place. But it was loose when I checked so it was even easier than usual. I may not have told you, but I believe Scott left the message there because he knew that was the sort of place I would look."

He had expected as much. "So you don't think the intruder left the message there and that maybe his gloves prevented him from popping the elevator back into place properly. You said he was wearing gloves, right?"

She nodded. "He was. For sure."

She rubbed at her arms, and he wrestled with the need to reach out and touch her, give her hand a reassuring squeeze…something to underscore she wasn't alone in this.

"Then it's reasonable to assume," he went on, pushing past the idea of touching her, "that the intruder who left the message in your garage could have left this message as well. The gloves and his haste left it loose, as you say. You never noticed it being loose before, did you?"

She thought about it for a moment, her expression shifting as if some realization had just dawned. "You're right… If it had been loose before, Janey would have noticed and wanted me to fix it. So it had to be him—the intruder." Shock flared in her eyes. "Oh. My. God." Her head moved slowly from side to side. "That means the intruder had to be him. Son of a…"

"Scott," Ben said. It wasn't a guess…it was a given.

She laughed out loud. "I can't believe I didn't consider that. The height was about right…the eye color. But it happened so quickly I didn't get a really good look. He shoved me against the wall, which sent me tumbling to the floor." She swore under her breath. "You must think I'm such a fool."

"You are not a fool, Brenda," he urged. "You had no reason to suspect it was him."

"But it had to be." She shook her head again.

"It's a possibility we can't rule out," he agreed. "Now the question is, why play this game? Obviously you and the bad guys both know he's still alive. It's not like he pulled that one off."

"He wasn't wearing the cologne he always wears," she said, uncertainty obviously poking its way into her thoughts.

"Then it's possible," Ben felt the need to say, "it wasn't him. But someone with whom he has shared details about you. Or maybe someone he hired and provided specific directions."

She lifted her gaze to his. "Maybe the blonde I saw him with at LAX."

"Maybe." He opted not to point out that she'd insisted the intruder was a man.

She made a face. "No. It was definitely a man." She turned fully to Ben. "I want to go to his house. I want to see inside. If there's something else the police aren't telling me, I need to know. I have a right to know. Maybe someone has been leaving messages there too."

"We're both aware that his home is a secondary crime scene and most likely sealed." Ben felt compelled to offer the warning.

"I don't care. Legally I'm still married to him so that

gives me the right to go into his home in his absence—at least in my mind."

He didn't argue. On a level the law wouldn't recognize, she considered herself entitled to this opportunity. She needed to be able to protect herself. She couldn't do that as long as she was left in the dark. "Point me in the right direction."

"Go back out to Triana Boulevard and take a right." As he drove, she said, "Tell me about this Jalisco cartel."

None of the information she'd just requested was going to make her feel better, but it wasn't as if she couldn't google it. "Extremely violent. Truly the worst of the worst. They have built a reputation as a new generation–style operation. Very diverse in their activities. Drugs. Human trafficking. Assassinations."

"Dear God. What was he thinking?" She shivered at the images his words no doubt prompted. "You need to take a left at the next intersection."

He slowed for the turn. "Not that I'm cutting him any slack," Ben pointed out before saying more, "but I doubt a lot of rational thought went into the decision. These kinds of moves typically happen just before things are about to fall apart. Desperation drives the decision."

"Whatever his motive," she contended, "his decision to leave us with this nightmare is unforgivable."

"Absolutely." There was no way to disagree with that conclusion.

While she simmered about the man's bad decisions, Ben focused on navigating the heavier traffic in the retail area along Airport Road. All those emotions she had attempted to keep under control the past couple of days were getting the better of her. Understandably so. It was the ultimate betrayal. Her husband had cheated repeatedly, then he'd left her in a dangerous situation with seemingly no way out. His one good deed was calling the Colby Agency.

"I want you to know," she spoke up after a couple of minutes of silence, "that all these emotions I'm dealing with aren't about me and certainly not about what Scott and I once had. All of what I'm feeling is because I'm worried about my little girl. One way or the other she has lost her father. I'm not seeing a way clear of it, and I'm terrified for her future."

He braked for a traffic signal and looked directly at her. "You don't need to worry about a way out of this, Brenda. That's my job, and you have my word you will get through this and safely to the other side of this nightmare."

She tried to smile but it didn't happen. Rather, she stared straight ahead. "Just promise me if there's no way to the other side for me that you'll keep my daughter safe."

This time he put his hand over hers and squeezed. "You and Janey will both be safe."

The light changed to green and he rolled forward.

"Ah…you should go…" She cleared her throat, swiped at her eyes with her free hand. "Left at the next light. You'll have to stop at the guard shack. I'll show my ID."

The next left took them onto Ledges Drive. At the guard shack, Ben stopped and powered down his window.

Brenda leaned toward him so that the guard could see her. "Hi. I'm Brenda Devers." She passed her driver's license to the man. "I'm going to my husband Scott Devers's house on Ledge View Drive."

"One moment." The man in the uniform returned her license, stepped back into the guard shack and checked whatever he needed to, then raised the gate and motioned for them to drive through.

Brenda relaxed into her seat once more.

Ben focused on the road as it wound up the mountainside, rising to the top and rolling into an elite housing development.

"Do you have a key?"

"Yes. I've only been here a couple of times, but he gave me one. For Janey, I guess. Just keep following Ledges Drive until you reach Ledge View, then turn right. After that it's the first house on the left."

The houses were large, the lots estate sized. Ben wasn't surprised. Scott Devers had a history of living large. He liked excessively expensive sports cars and, clearly, elegant mansions surrounded by other elegant mansions. The contrast between him and Brenda was stunning.

"Turn into the driveway and I'll get out and open the garage door."

Ben followed her instructions, waiting with the engine running as she entered the code for one of three garage doors. When it opened, she stepped aside and motioned for him to pull inside. Smart decision. It was better to avoid being noticed if possible.

Once he was inside, he shifted into Park and shut off the engine. The door closed behind him. As he emerged, he noted the workout area in one of the other bays. All state-of-the-art equipment. In the third bay was a vintage Porsche. Again, Ben noted the astounding difference between Scott and Brenda.

Brenda waited at the entrance door to the house.

"I assume you have the security code in case the alarm is activated."

She nodded. "I do." She unlocked the door and walked in.

Ben stayed close behind her. The house was dark save for lights from appliances and electronics and the meager remaining daylight filtering through the plantation shutters. Quiet too. No signal the alarm required a code.

"I guess the police called for the alarm to be turned off," she said. "They certainly didn't call me asking for a code."

"That's the usual protocol," Ben offered. "I should go first as we walk through."

She waited for him to walk past her. He used the flashlight app on his phone as he went. Just enough extra light to see clearly. No need to alert the neighbors.

The kitchen was large, modern. Lots of gleaming white and polished stainless steel. High-end commercial-grade appliances the man likely never used. Rich hardwood floors. Posh furniture.

They moved beyond the dining room into the massive great room with its view looking out over the infinity pool and the cliffs behind the house. The sun was fading, sending long shadows across the treetops.

"Any place in particular you believe we should look?" Signs the police had done their work were everywhere. They had taken the place and everything inside it apart.

She surveyed the chaos. "You mean someplace they haven't already looked?"

He laughed, or attempted to. "If such a place exists, yes."

"I suppose we can just keep going from room to room and maybe something will pop out at me."

Room by room, they plowed through the mess left by the official search. Then up the grand staircase to the bedrooms, where they did the same there. They checked for hidden places in souvenirs Scott had purchased in South America on one of his many trips. But none had secret openings or false bottoms.

If the man had any evidence hidden here, it was long

gone. They found nothing. No messages written on the walls. Not one thing.

Outside on the rear patio, Brenda stared out over the lights below. Darkness had fallen, so the lights from the city in the valley beneath them were all there was to see, other than a few stars overhead. Gas streetlamps flickered along Ledge View Drive, but their glow was dim. He suspected not diminishing the starlight was the point.

"We should go," he suggested. There was nothing more to do here.

She had to be exhausted, emotionally and physically.

"This was what he always wanted." She turned to Ben. "This glamorous lifestyle. Bragging rights."

Scott Devers had grown up a poor kid on a farm in the tiny community of Princeton, Alabama. He'd done well for himself…until a couple of years ago.

But money hadn't been his only obsession.

Ben's attention settled on the woman standing so close. Her husband hadn't appreciated her…hadn't respected her. That, in Ben's opinion, was where his long line of bad choices had begun.

She gazed out over the valley below once more. "I hope for Janey's sake he doesn't end up dead again. I don't want to have to explain that to her."

"What's going on here?"

He and Brenda turned simultaneously at the firm demand.

Special Agent Cummings, flanked by two uniformed Huntsville PD officers, stood in the expansive open space created by the foldaway glass wall of doors.

"Ms. Devers," he said, "Mr. Clark, perhaps you're unaware that this is a secondary crime scene. The front door was sealed. Did you not see the seal?"

Brenda stepped forward before Ben could respond. "We came in through the garage. That's the way I've always come into my *husband's* home."

"Then I suppose we can let this misstep go, but I'm sure Detective Shelton will be speaking with you about the rules related to crime scenes."

"Why are you here, Agent Cummings?" She surveyed the three men.

She was angry now. Ben didn't blame her. She'd been through enough to be outraged.

"Huntsville PD received a call from a neighbor that lights had come on in the house," Cummings explained. "I'm staying nearby and came right away, but I waited for the officers to arrive before entering the house."

"Nearby?" A frown tugged at Brenda's face. "Where? I know the area well."

"With a friend." He looked to Ben. "We should get the house locked up."

Ben recognized his cue to act. He touched Brenda's arm. "We'll be on our way then." Inside, he hesitated. "I'm assuming you have no news about the case." When the other man failed to answer immediately, Ben tacked on, "I'm confident you're keeping Ms. Devers fully and promptly informed since her safety is involved."

"Of course." Cummings smiled, but it was as false as his answer. "There is no news to report."

Ben smiled back and then he and Brenda walked away. He wondered though why the agent had chosen to lie.

Chapter Twelve

Devers Residence
White Street
Huntsville, 7:45 p.m.

Brenda was tremendously relieved when Ben parked in the garage behind her house. No matter that an intruder had invaded her private space and planted a bomb to harm or, at the very least, scare her, this was home and she was glad to be home.

On the drive back to Five Points, Detective Shelton had called to inform Brenda that her property had been released. The explosion was in the alley behind her detached garage, so there was no reason to hold her home or the garage hostage any longer. *Hostage* was her word, not his. But at this point she felt as if she were being held hostage by whatever Scott had left them with.

The mere notion that he was alive and out there somewhere hiding while she endured this escalating travesty infuriated her.

Ben shut off the engine and turned to her. "When we go inside, let's not talk until I've had a look around."

Her gaze narrowed. "Does this have something to do with why you examined my cell phone when we got in the car to leave Scott's house?"

He nodded. "I got the distinct impression that Agent Cummings was not being entirely forthcoming with us. It might be nothing but better to be safe than sorry."

"Agreed."

Brenda wondered as she emerged from Ben's car if he'd ever spent this much time dedicated to an assignment. He'd been her new neighbor for a little over two weeks. If he was married, his wife probably thought he was never coming home.

After they exited the garage, she studied the man who walked ahead of her to the back door. He seemed completely at ease with the length of time he'd been on the job here. He glanced back and repeated that he should take a look inside before she went in. All of this, she reminded herself, was just part of the job. He was clearly not just an investigator. He was a bodyguard.

A bodyguard. The idea made her head spin. Not even one of her heroines had ever required a bodyguard. None had ever been the target of a bomb either. She might have to step up her plotting game after this. The research was certainly done.

She waited on the back patio while he unlocked the door, deactivated the alarm and walked deeper into the house. Leaning against the doorframe, she considered that he didn't wear a wedding band. Never mentioned a wife or girlfriend. But then, maybe it was policy not to discuss his private life. Lots of people didn't wear jewelry at all. The missing band didn't mean anything.

Still, a guy as nice and as good-looking as Ben Clark likely had a girlfriend. She was thirty-one. He was surely her age or a little older.

"The house is clear."

The sound of his voice startled her, and she jumped as

if he'd walked up and said *boo*. Her face flushed, which made her immensely thankful the light by the back door was not on.

"Thanks." She went inside, moving past him in hopes he wouldn't notice her embarrassment. No reason to beat herself up for being distracted. The past two days had been hardcore stressful. Her mind and body were likely seeking release anywhere it could be found. The thought of release had her mind going other places that she had not been in about a year. Places she did not need to go under current circumstances.

"You want to order pizza or something?" he asked.

She dropped her handbag on the bench by the back door and turned to answer, only to find he was standing right next to her. She jumped again, couldn't suppress the reaction. She really had to get herself together here.

He showed her his cell phone screen, where he'd typed a message but hadn't hit Send.

Going next door for something. Be right back. Order pizza.

She nodded and said, "Pizza works for me. I'm thinking pepperoni."

"Add olives, okay?" he said as he headed out the door.

"Sure."

He slipped out the back door without a sound and left it partially open. She made her way to the window and watched him hurry through the near darkness. The shrubs and trees of her yard cast the neighboring house in deep shadows. Since there was only one streetlamp on this end of the alley, it was mostly dark too. She walked to the living room and checked out the front window in an attempt to see if that black sedan was still parked on the street. She should have asked Agent Cummings if he had someone watching her. She supposed he did. If not him, maybe Detective Shelton. After all, she was a suspect.

She walked back to the kitchen and made the call to the pizza shop a couple of streets over on Andrew Jackson Way. Making a call rather than placing the order online would help to fill the silence until Ben was back. The hold time had her wondering if she should carry on a pretend conversation.

"I'll order soft drinks too," she said aloud.

"You have ice?"

She jumped. Jeez, she had to stop doing that. She shot Ben a wide-eyed look that loudly exclaimed that he'd scared her half to death—again. "I do," she said, instead of warning that her heart couldn't take any more.

He gave her a contrite look and pressed a hand to his chest as if apologizing.

His reaction stirred one in her, made her want to feel his arms around her again.

Thankfully the crew member's voice echoed in her ear just then. With too much of her attention still on Ben in the kitchen getting ice, then water in a glass, she somehow managed to place the order and end the call.

"Pizza will be here in half an hour."

"Can't wait." He patted his lean waist. "I'm starving."

She was too. She blinked, scrambled for something to say. She started to ask if she should round him up something to snack on to go with the water, but she reconsidered, realizing he was probably just making small talk. She really, really had to get her head on straight here.

When he started what looked like a new search of some sort, she wandered over and started to follow him. They moved around the living room as he checked under lampshades, in and around electric outlets, under tables and basically about everywhere. Once, then again, and again he removed something tiny—barely the size of a dime—and dropped it into the water.

The whole time he talked…about the weather…about anything and everything.

Then she got it. Her mouth fell slack. No matter that earlier today they'd been through the whole house, they hadn't been looking for tiny items that might look like a button or a spot on the fabric but were actually listening devices. Another went into the glass of ice water. The scene was like something from a spy movie. Brenda had actually read about clear listening devices—like little slips of tape—making them invisible once they were in place on a person or thing.

He made a rolling motion with his hand. Shoot, she was supposed to be doing the small-talk thing to disguise what they were doing. He'd done his share. Now it was her turn apparently.

She said, "You have family back home?" Since she'd allowed the silence to drag on too long, the sound of her own voice startled her. Or maybe it was the fact that he'd had to prompt her.

Sheesh, Brenda, you had this one job and you allowed distraction to get in the way.

Some spy she would make.

"I do." He glanced at her and smiled. "My folks live in Naperville."

She got stuck on that smile. He had the…most intriguing smile. Nice, but something more. Sexy. Yes, she decided. Very sexy.

"You?" he prompted.

There there she went again, getting distracted. "My parents," she said so fast the words almost came out as one, "were older when they had me. Sadly, they died when I was in college. I so regret they never got to meet Janey."

Her sweet baby girl. Janey was what she should be thinking about now…not whatever this relentless urge was that kept tugging at her. She cleared her head and focused on the man whose job it was to be here doing what he was doing. This wasn't personal and it certainly wasn't intimate.

He considered her for a moment as if he'd read her thoughts. "That must have been a tough time for you."

"Yes. My mother died first. She'd had heart surgery, but things didn't go so well. There were complications, but no one realized until it was too late. Anyway, she was doing what she loved most—working in her flower garden. Janey is named after her."

Ben smiled. "What about your father?"

"Dad was as healthy as a horse. I think he died from a broken heart. The two of them had been together for more than half their lives." A smile tugged at the corners of her mouth as she thought of her parents. "Their relationship was the kind every couple should have. The sort of love you read about in romance novels. Deep respect for one another. They were amazing."

"They sound like my parents." That sexy smile was back. "Totally committed to each other. I wonder sometimes how it's possible to love someone that much. It seems all-consuming."

"God knows I haven't figured it out," she admitted. "I thought I had but I was wrong."

He didn't ask her to expand on the comment, and she was grateful. She could have left that part off.

They moved on to the kitchen. She didn't actually have a dining room. The previous owners had sacrificed it to make a larger living room with a wide cased opening that led into the kitchen. Worked out fine for Brenda. She wasn't a formal table kind of person. She and Janey generally used the island.

"We're young," he reminded her, drawing her back to the conversation. "We still have time to find the right people to share our lives with."

Watching his hands touch each item he reached for was almost as hypnotic as watching his lips move. She blinked and silently chastised herself. She must really be desperate for stress relief. There were plenty of reasons why she needed it, but this was not the time.

The thing he'd said about how they still had time penetrated all the other static in her head. Did that mean he was single? *Doesn't matter.*

"You have siblings?" she asked, when she really wanted to inquire about his relationship status. *Not going there.*

"Three brothers. All older."

"So you're the baby?" Interesting.

He laughed. "Thirty-two is hardly a baby, but yeah, I guess I am." He motioned for her to follow him into the hall. "What about you?"

He already knew this answer. The Colby Agency had likely done a thorough background search on her. "No one else. Just me. I believe my mother said they'd given up hope of ever having children and suddenly I came along."

He checked Janey's room, the bathroom and her office and then moved on to her bedroom. It suddenly felt too intimate having him run his fingers over her things, even though he'd already been through her room before. She lingered at the door, deciding not getting too close was the best choice at the moment.

He leaned forward, checked the lamp on her side of the bed. Then he crouched down and examined her bedside table. When he stood, she watched far too closely the way he moved. His long legs, lean body…broad shoulders. Her throat went dry.

She gave herself a mental kick. This was beyond ridiculous. He hadn't mentioned a significant other but that didn't mean—

"You didn't ask—" he leaned against her dresser and studied her "—if I was with anyone."

For two beats she struggled to figure out how to respond. "I figured if you wanted me to know you would tell me." *Perfect.*

"In case you wondered, the answer is no. I was engaged once, years ago, but that didn't work out. We're still friends, but she's married to someone else and has two cute kids."

Brenda wondered what woman in her right mind would toss this guy aside. But then she barely knew him. He might not be… What was she thinking, of course he was. He was really nice, inordinately handsome. Ugh. *Stop!*

He pushed off the dresser and started her way. Her breath caught. Okay, enough of this fantasy. She recognized the need for distraction, but this was not the way to assuage all the emotions twisting inside her.

The doorbell sounded, and she had never been so relieved in her life. She headed that way. "Must be the pizza," she called out as she practically ran.

Somehow Ben reached the door before her and took care of the tab and the tip.

Brenda went back into the kitchen and slid onto a stool, rested her elbow on the counter and stared at the glass with the tiny electronic devices floating amid the melting ice cubes. Whoever put those in her home was convinced she knew something. Why would anyone believe this when she had never been involved with Scott's business? Unless he told the bad guys—and these were really bad guys—otherwise. If she got her hands on him…

Ben placed the box and the drinks next to the glass. "You have paper plates?"

"I do. They're an essential around here." She reached over and opened one of the drawers on the island. She liked keeping paper plates handy. They were immensely useful for snacking children. Not to mention they were unbreakable. Whenever Janey had friends over, paper plates were the preferred dishware.

The fresh wave of feelings came from deep inside so quickly and with such impact, she couldn't hope to slow them. Would she ever have a normal evening with her daughter again? Here in their home? How could the man she had once loved and married—for God's sake—have allowed this to happen?

Forget about his wife, why would he let this happen to his own child?

No, the real question was, how had *she* allowed this to happen? Why hadn't she paid better attention?

How had she become so complacent?

"Go ahead and start without me." She placed the plates on the counter. "I should call Janey before her bedtime."

She backed away, then turned and hurried to her room. She put through a call to Mallory's number. The call was answered on the second ring.

"Hey, Brenda, is everything okay?"

"Yeah." She sat down on the edge of her bed, an urgency pulsing inside her. "I just need to hear Janey's voice."

"Oh." Mallory made a sound of regret. "She's asleep already. Would you like me to wake her? That little girl is really missing you too. She keeps asking when we can go home."

The words pierced right through the center of Brenda's chest. "No. Don't wake her." Just because she was miserable didn't mean Janey had to be as well. "I'll call her in the morning."

"Are you all right, Brenda? We've been worried about you."

"Yeah. I guess I am. I'm just tired and missing my child."

"My word," Mallory said. "After all you've been through it's no wonder you're tired. Most people would be hiding in their closets sucking their thumbs about now. You should be proud of the strength you've shown, Brenda."

She wasn't feeling particularly proud or strong right now.

"The one thing you don't have to worry about," Mallory went on, "is your daughter. She's fine. She misses you but she's fine."

"Thank you. I really miss her."

"'Course you do."

A second or two of silence and then Mallory asked, "So you've found nothing that might be whatever that message on your garage door was about?"

"Not one thing." She decided not to tell Mallory about the message on Bradley Street or the visit to Scott's house. What was the point? They had learned nothing. Everywhere they looked there was either nothing or some dead-end lead.

"I'm really sorry this is happening. Please let me know if there's anything else we can do."

Brenda smiled sadly. "Just take care of my little girl."

"You got it."

They said their goodbyes and Brenda ended the call. She should take a shower and just go to bed. Who wanted pizza again? What had she been thinking ordering it? But then if she did go to bed and managed to sleep she would only have bad dreams. Better to stay awake until she was too exhausted to dream.

A soft rap on the open door had her shifting her attention there.

"Pizza's getting cold." He studied her closely. "You okay?"

Brenda pushed to her feet and walked toward him, unsure if she could work up an appetite. Especially for pizza. "I spoke to Mallory."

He stepped aside for her to pass. "Everything okay?"

"She said everything is fine and that I shouldn't worry."

"Easier said than done." He followed her to the kitchen.

Brenda put a slice of pizza on a paper plate and picked at it, the idea of taking an actual bite making her queasy. "I keep asking myself where else Scott would hide anything in my house. I mean, we're assuming he wrote that address on the Barbie elevator, but what if he wasn't the intruder?"

"Taking a broader look, the one issue I'm having with him being the intruder is why—if he hid something—threaten you to find it for him? He would know where it was. And if his goal was to give you clues to its location, why all the subterfuge?"

"That's a very good point." She did take a bite of the cheesy pepperoni pie then. The nibbles had roused her appetite. "Off and on all day I've been mulling over where he would have hidden something so important or valuable to the cartel."

"That is the one point," Ben offered, "I believe we can safely assume without question. Scott has something they want. Depending on what exactly it is—files, a storage device of some sort—it would likely need to stay dry. Safe from fire. And, obviously, hidden somewhere we haven't looked."

"Given we and the police have gone through this place

with no luck it has to be a really good place." God, she was so sick of this mess.

Maybe it wasn't even in the house. She thought of the flowerpots on the patio that the intruder had pilfered through. But if Scott was the intruder, was all that for show? No doubt the police had gone through those as well, maybe with just a tad more care for the plants. She needed to take care of that jumble of potting soil and abused plants. Good thing they hadn't dug around in the ones in her home. Her attention rested on the snake plant sitting in the white porcelain pot next to the sink. That would really have been a mess.

But why hadn't they? Even if the police hadn't, why didn't the intruder dig around in that plant? He'd gone through the ones on the patio. She left the half-eaten pizza on the now greasy paper plate and walked over to the sink. She stared at the potting soil for a moment. It looked undisturbed. Then she touched it, scratched around. The surface was firm enough she felt sure it hadn't been recently disturbed. So she moved on to the philodendron in the turquoise pot next to it. Soil looked undisturbed. Surface was firm to the touch.

The only other indoor plants were in the bathroom, she considered, her feet already taking her in that direction.

Another philodendron and a fern. The fern was her favorite. Nothing disturbed in the philodendron. Disappointment tagged her when she felt around the base of the fern. The soil around it felt firm and undisturbed as well. She stood back a moment, stared at the two plants. But there was a difference between the fern and all the other plants. The philodendrons and the snake plant were in pots with built-in saucers for drainage. The vintage terra-cotta pot the fern was in had a separate drain saucer.

It was a long shot, but she might as well look.

Holding her breath, Brenda picked up the pot. The saucer was stuck, so, with effort, she tugged until she pulled it free. Right there stuck in the saucer was what appeared to be a piece of folded plastic with something white inside. It was hard to tell since the water that had seeped from the drain hole had stained and yellowed the plastic. Obviously, whatever this was, it had been here for a while.

Heart thudding like a drum, she pulled the plastic free. Not plain plastic, a sandwich bag. Fingers fumbling, she unfolded it and pulled the plastic open then reached into the bag.

"Ben!" She held the paper with the tips of two fingers, too afraid to open it for fear of somehow damaging whatever it was. There were darker areas in the folds that made her think there were written or typed words on the paper.

Ben appeared at the door.

She held up the paper. "This was stuck inside the drain saucer under that fern. If they picked up the pot, they probably thought it didn't come apart since none of the other pots do. But it does, it just took some effort." Who would have thought anything of it…save for her—the person who bought it. This vintage pot was her favorite. She found it at a flea market in Chelsea on one of her trips to New York forever ago. Scott had been with her.

Her gaze met Ben's, and she asked, anticipation making it hard to breathe, "Do you think this is what we've been looking for?"

Chapter Thirteen

9:25 p.m.

Ben stared at the piece of paper and his lips spread into a grin. “I think maybe you’ve found it.”

Could be an old girlfriend’s details, but Ben’s instincts were humming. This had to be the *it* that was causing all the mayhem.

It wasn’t that large. Maybe three inches by three inches. But it was folded at least once. He took the paper from her and placed it on the counter. “You have tweezers?”

“Somewhere.” She pulled out a drawer and prowled through it. “Here you go.” She extended the tweezers toward him. She was breathless with anticipation. He had to admit to feeling a bit like that himself.

He hoped this wasn’t going to be another letdown, but he suspected that was not the case.

Being as careful as possible, he picked at one corner until the top layer came free of the one beneath it. Using his forefinger to hold the paper down, he slowly drew back the fold. Then he did the same with the next one. As he’d estimated, the page turned out to be about a six-by-six that had been folded in half in two directions. On the paper, written in two columns on the top half, were three names. Beneath those were three series of numbers.

"That's his handwriting." Brenda's eyes were bright with rising emotion.

"Do you recognize any of the names?" He pulled out his cell phone and snapped a pic in case the paper got damaged or stolen. At this point there was no way to know when the police or someone else would barge in.

She scrutinized the list. "I don't. No. Do you think this has been hidden here for a long while?"

"I think—" he refolded the paper "—we can safely assume it has been here since he started talking to the Bureau." He tucked the paper back into the bag and handed it to her. "Put that somewhere you think no one will look."

She grinned. "I know just the place." She picked up the fern and placed it back in the saucer. "I think it'll be safe there."

He chuckled. "I think you're right."

"Can someone at your agency figure out who those people are?"

"They can. I'll send the photo to a colleague."

He led the way back to the kitchen. She settled on a stool, propped her elbows on the counter and set her head in her hands. It was easy to see that she was exhausted and emotionally drained. He wished there was a way to make this easier for her.

If they were lucky, this could be the moment where things turned around. He leaned against the island and sent the image to the expert, Max Granger, in tracking down accounts and the electronic trails left by people. Then he googled the first name on the found list. The search showed that the man lived in the Huntsville area. Ben took a screenshot of the information. Then he moved on to the next. It took a minute, but he found Huntsville area addresses on all three.

He swiped through the screenshots, giving Brenda time to consider each one. "Anything seem familiar?"

She inspected each image, her face a study in concentration. He wondered if she had any idea how good she looked in nothing more complicated than jeans and a sweatshirt. He liked that she wore her hair down, loose around her shoulders. She looked so young. He wanted desperately to protect her, but he was also well aware of how strong she was.

She shook her head. "I mean, I know where these areas are, but I don't know the people."

"He never talked about the firm's clients?"

She sipped her soft drink. "He used to mention whenever they landed big deals or managed some particularly important accomplishment, but that was years ago. He really didn't talk much about work around me the past couple of years." She made a face as if she were concentrating hard to recall something. "It was when Janey was about two, I think, he mentioned something to the effect that everything was about to change for the better. The firm was expanding. He and Tate wanted to play with the big boys." She shook her head as if shaking off a strange moment. "I'd completely forgotten about that until now."

"It's likely that was when the two started talking to someone who pulled them into the darkness."

"That's a good way to put it." She folded her arms over her chest. "To my knowledge the firm was doing just fine at the time. So the move was about bigger money and more power, I suspect. He took the risk for all the wrong reasons."

"Some do. For others it's about desperation."

"What do you make of those numbers?"

"Routing numbers for accounts, I'm guessing. I've sent

the information to a colleague who specializes in tracing accounts. Whatever there is to find, he'll find it."

"Thank you. Again." Brenda peered up at him. "I really don't know what I would have done if you hadn't been here."

"Don't thank me," he warned. "We're not out of the woods yet."

She suddenly slid off the stool and went on tiptoe to hug him. The move was so unexpected, for a moment he could only stand there. Then his arms went around her and he hugged her back. Her petite body felt good against his. He closed his eyes and relished the sensation of having her in his arms. It was not a smart move, but it was one he couldn't resist. He liked her…a lot.

She drew back just enough to look into his eyes. "I know this is probably a mistake, but fair warning, I can't…"

He kissed her. Whatever the hell had gotten into him, he couldn't name. Call it lust…call it whatever, but he needed to kiss her. To somehow make her feel safe and appreciated… wanted.

She melted more firmly against him…kissed him with a ferocity that set him on fire.

The doorbell went off, the sound echoing through the house.

They drew apart just as quickly as they had come together.

"I'll get it," she said before rushing away.

The loss of her body against his made him slump with frustration. Pulling himself together, he followed the path she had taken.

"Check the peephole," he reminded her when she would have opened the door. His voice sounded overly coarse, but there was no help for it.

She turned to him. "It's Agent Cummings."

The heat and desire that had taken over drained out of him. "Good. We need to speak with him."

Looking confused, she opened the door. "Agent Cummings, has something else happened?"

They'd seen him just a couple of hours ago at Scott Devers's house.

"May I come in?" the agent asked, looking from Brenda to Ben and back. The suspicion on his face blatant. Glaring.

Ben knew exactly what that was about.

While Brenda invited him in, Ben went to the kitchen. He picked up the glass and walked back to where Brenda was offering the man a seat.

"I don't have a lot of time," Cummings was saying, ignoring the offered seat. "I just stopped by to ensure that you're all right. You seemed upset when we spoke earlier."

Before Brenda could respond, Ben handed him the glass of water. The ice had all melted and the little electronic devices were blatantly visible.

"I think these belong to you."

Cummings accepted the glass and stared into it, then glowered at Ben. "Where did you find these?"

"Right where you or Detective Shelton planted them."

Since his reaction lacked one iota of outrage, the answer to who was responsible for the potentially illegal intrusion was standing right in front of them. The listening devices belonged to Cummings.

Ben stepped to the door, opened it. "It's late, Agent Cummings. We should talk tomorrow."

Clearly flustered now, Cummings did an about-face and walked out, taking the glass with him. Ben closed and locked the door behind him.

He made a face. "I hope you weren't attached to that glass."

Brenda laughed. “I am not, and even if I were, it was worth letting it go to watch his reaction.”

Ben moved closer to her. “I think we were in the middle of something when Cummings showed up.”

“I seem to recall there was a little something happening,” she agreed, moving in a little closer.

His arms went around her, but he didn’t restart the kiss. First he had to know. “We don’t have to do this. Tonight’s find is cause for celebration, for sure. But we don’t—”

She shut him up with her mouth.

So they celebrated…and he showed her how a man who respected a woman, who treasured their intimacy made love.

Chapter Fourteen

Thursday, May 7
Winthrop Residence
Eagle Ridge Place
Huntsville, 8:30 a.m.

Brenda kept her focus straight ahead as they started up the sidewalk. Waking up to the sound of the shower and Ben's scent on her sheets had been…revitalizing in several ways. But, at the same time, it was terrifying. Had she made a mistake? Should she have allowed pleasure to slip into their relationship?

Pleasure was a very apt description. She had never been made to feel the way this man made her feel. She stole a glance at him from the corner of her eye. And he'd been such a gentleman this morning. Since he was in the shower when she woke, that first awkward moment of waking together was prevented. Then, before she'd talked herself into climbing out of bed, he'd headed to the kitchen and started preparing breakfast. Again, ensuring she was able to shower and dress before the unavoidable morning-after face-to-face moment.

Even more surprising, he had somehow made her feel instantly at ease during breakfast. He'd talked about the case and the next steps and even the weather. She hadn't felt pressured to discuss their night spent in each other's arms. No need to analyze what it meant or whether it would happen again.

The perfect morning after.

Another glance at him and she admitted that a lot of things about Ben Clark were perfect. The angles of his face. His smile. Those eyes. She liked that he wore jeans with his sports jackets. He looked at ease and confident. Totally comfortable in his own skin. Truth was, there were a lot things about him that she liked…a whole lot.

"Would you like me to ask the questions?"

Brenda blinked. A moment was required to figure out what he meant. The interview of the first name on the list they'd found. Further proof that last night had been good for her. Her mind wasn't trapped in that continuous loop replaying the nightmare her life had become.

"Yes. I'm glad you asked. I would very much appreciate your taking the lead." After all, he was the expert. No matter that she'd conducted a few interrogations and interviews in her books, this was real life. She would prefer to leave it to the experienced expert.

He smiled in her direction. "Good. You study his reactions, and we'll have a postmortem after."

"That's a great idea." She faced forward. Maybe today they would make some real headway on solving this puzzle.

The Winthrop home was a stately one. The owner, Albert Winthrop, was the first name on the list they had found last night. Hopefully, he would have some sort of answers for them. Whoever was behind the threats against her would be growing impatient. She needed to find what they wanted. It would certainly be a lot easier if she had some idea what *it* was. The location of money…drugs…information that could be used against them?

At the front door, Ben pressed the button for the doorbell. Brenda stood slightly back. This man was older, mid-seventies. According to Google, he was a widower. She didn't want him to feel intimidated by the two of them arriving unannounced.

The door opened, but it wasn't the elderly man whose image they had found on the internet. This was a woman, perhaps a year or so older than Brenda.

"Good morning," Ben said. "My name is Ben Clark. I'm from the Colby Agency and this is my colleague, Brenda. We're here to speak with Mr. Winthrop."

Brenda recognized instantly that something was very wrong. The woman's eyes were red, and while Ben spoke they filled with tears and her lips trembled ever so slightly.

"I apologize for the intrusion," he offered. "If this is a bad time, we can come back later."

Brenda held her breath. They needed answers now, not later. But Ben was right to make the offer.

"My father," the woman said, then hesitated to take a deep breath, "died last night."

Fear poked into Brenda's gut, but she quickly found her voice and offered, "I'm so sorry for your loss." Disappointment sagged her shoulders because she did not want to lose this opportunity, as selfish as that sounded. But if the man was dead…what could they do?

The woman nodded. "Thank you." Then she frowned. "Was my father expecting you? I'm not familiar with the Colby Agency."

Brenda looked to Ben for the answer on that one.

"No," Ben explained. "He wasn't expecting us, but we

found his name on a list related to J&D Investments, and we're trying to narrow down—"

A sad laugh burst out of the woman. "I don't think you would have wanted to hear what he had to say about the people who operated that firm."

Brenda couldn't hold back. "Scott Devers was my husband," she explained. "I'm desperate to determine what was actually going on before the explosion. If you could help I would sincerely appreciate it."

The other woman's face hardened, but Brenda kept going. "Scott and I had been separated for a year, which is why I have no idea about his business dealings. All I know for certain is that whatever he was doing, now my daughter and I are in danger. That's why we wanted to talk to Mr. Winthrop. I hoped he might be able to shed some light on the situation."

Her face softened a little. "I'm very sorry for whatever you and your daughter are going through. All I know is that my father discovered millions of dollars were missing from his accounts. He'd had hip and knee replacement surgery and then spent weeks in a rehab facility. During that time the money disappeared. Once he was home and back to monitoring his business affairs, he found the discrepancies."

"What was the time frame that he made the discovery?" Ben asked.

"About a month ago."

"What did he do once he realized what was happening?" Ben inquired next.

"He confronted Scott Devers. But Scott claimed it was just a mistake in the reporting system, that the money was right where it was supposed to be. Then magically within twenty-four hours the money showed up—just like he said. My father went to a friend whose accountant specializes in forensic auditing, and he took a look and said there was only one explanation for what my father described. The money was being used illegally. A day or so later, I think, the explosion happened."

Ben said, "Did your father go to the authorities?"

"Oh yeah. A detective…" She narrowed her gaze as if concentrating on recalling the name. "Sheldon or Shelton, I think he said. Anyway, the detective took his statement, but we never heard anything else."

Brenda felt like she needed to apologize for Scott's actions, but then his choices had not been hers. Still, it was painful to hear the story.

"Ms. Winthrop?" Ben asked.

"Bowden," she clarified. "Tess Bowden."

"I realize how difficult this must be," he said, "but would you mind sharing what happened to your father?"

Bowden squeezed her eyes shut for a moment. "He came to my house for dinner last night. I live in the Green Mountain community, and I didn't want him to drive home afterward. It was dark and the road is full of sharp curves." Her voice trembled on the last word. "But he insisted. At this point, all we know is that he missed a curve. But the police assured me they are conducting a thorough investigation. They're doing an autopsy to see if a medical event caused the accident. Whatever caused it, I want to know."

"No other vehicles were involved?" Ben asked.

"If anyone else was involved, they drove on without stopping or calling for help."

The idea that the accident was possibly no accident had dread creeping up Brenda's spine, twisting at the base of her skull. The thought might not have occurred to her except for what Ben had warned this cartel was capable of.

What the hell had Scott been thinking?

"Do you know if your father's funds remained where they should be?"

Brenda couldn't help holding her breath while waiting for the answer to Ben's question. If Scott had cheated this family…

"Oh yes. My father moved them to a new firm immediately."

Ben took a business card from his jacket pocket and handed it to Bowden. "If you recall anything else your father might have said or if you have any problems related to this situation, don't hesitate to call."

She stared for a long moment at the card, then looked from Brenda to Ben. "Why would you help me?"

"Because the people Scott Devers was involved with are very dangerous," Ben explained. "Detective Shelton should have told you this. There is a Special Agent Cummings from the FBI working on the case as well. You should be very careful, Ms. Bowden."

She thanked them and closed the door as they walked away.

Brenda waited, her nerves jittery, while Ben checked his car before they could get inside. Then she dared to utter the question throbbing in her skull. "There are two more names on that list… Do you think we're going to find the same pattern with them as well?"

Ben checked the street and pulled away from the curb. "Unfortunately, I suspect so." He glanced at Brenda. "The real question in my mind is, why hasn't Shelton or Cummings done a deeper dig? Why hasn't one or both followed up with this woman?"

And that reality had only been the beginning, Brenda soon learned. The second name on the list was indeed a client of Scott's firm and he too was deceased. The truly bizarre part was that he had been dead for more than a year.

None of the neighbors at his address had any idea about surviving family or even friends. The home was empty, the maintenance taken care of by a local company called Home Corp. A trip to the office proved futile. The employee at the desk wouldn't discuss the specifics about who paid for the service. No matter that more than one neighbor insisted the owner whose name went with the address was deceased. One neighbor had even been home the evening the owner was taken away by the coroner—after a fall down the stairs.

A stop at county records downtown showed that the property was still owned by the name on the list Brenda had found. Taxes were paid promptly by the same maintenance company.

When they drove away from the courthouse, Brenda couldn't hold in the frustration any longer. "This is getting stranger and stranger. I'm a writer, and I can't even imagine what could happen next."

"Since we can't access the client records from J&D Investments," Ben said with a glance in her direction, "we can't confirm what we believe we've found with these two clients."

"Had they been killing people no one would miss so they could keep using their money?" Brenda blurted.

"That's a valid scenario," Ben agreed. "There's also the possibility the one death—from a year ago—was an accident and the firm took advantage of the situation. My colleague in Chicago is working on finding answers as well."

"What should we do with what we've uncovered?" Brenda wasn't sure what to do with the little bit that may or may not be evidence. Sadly, it didn't feel complete or concrete.

Ben made a turn based on the navigation app's directions to the home of the next and final name on the list. "I don't believe we can trust Shelton or Cummings with this information. For now, I think we wait and see what else we find."

"It's so strange not to be able to trust the people who are supposed to protect you." She'd had that feeling since this thing started.

"I'm not suggesting—" Ben glanced at her as he slowed for a traffic signal "—that the local police or the Bureau isn't doing its job or that either man is not a good cop. But I am suggesting that something is off in this investigation, and we need to proceed with caution."

"Maybe we'll have better luck with this last one." It would be nice if Luther Holland was alive…unlike the others. They needed to find something soon.

"If not," Ben reminded her, "we'll just keep digging."

A few more minutes and they arrived at the stately home on Alexander Drive. Brenda decided not to get her hopes up considering they'd gotten nothing that explained why these three names in particular had been hidden. Though Scott had obviously written the names and hidden that paper for a reason, they were no closer now than they were twenty-four hours ago to knowing what the bad guys wanted. It was like swimming in a circle. No matter how fast you swam, you never really went anywhere.

Like the others' addresses, the house looked well-kept. The neighborhood was high-end with homes in the seven-figure price range. Homes with residents who likely had the big bucks, as Mallory would say.

Brenda had dreamed of Janey last night. She'd been playing in the woods in the park on Monte Sano Mountain.

Brenda had been trying to catch up with her to warn that she was veering too close to the edge of the cliff, but she could never catch her. Her heart hurt even now with the memory.

Waking this morning after a night of lovemaking with Ben had prevented that nightmare from following her through the day so far. To say she felt immensely less stressed would be an understatement. What she felt—she smiled—was something more than simply relaxed. She felt good. Really good. Happy. As happy as anyone could feel considering her cheating, supposedly dead husband was actually alive and on the run and a drug cartel was threatening her. And that her sweet little girl was in hiding.

They had to find answers soon. Brenda didn't want to be apart from Janey longer than absolutely necessary.

At the door of the final location on their list, Ben pressed the button for the doorbell. It wasn't the usual old-fashioned doorbell. It was one of those with a camera built-in and the capability for communicating with the person or persons who lived in the house even if they weren't home.

"What do you want?"

The harsh words echoed from the little metal box attached to the wall next to the door.

Ben removed his credentials case and held it in front of the camera. "I'm Ben Clark from the Colby Agency—a private investigations firm out of Chicago. This is Brenda Devers. We're here to speak with—"

"Devers?" the man's voice snapped. "Any relation to Scott Devers?"

Brenda exchanged a look with Ben, then nodded. "Yes."

"Why are you here?" he demanded, his tone as much resigned now as angry.

"I'm trying to find someone who can help me figure out

what my husband did to have people threatening me and my daughter. We have no idea what's going on, but our lives are in danger." Tears burned her eyes, but she blinked them back. She would not cry, damn it.

"I can't invite you in," Mr. Holland explained, his tone calmer, "because I'm not home. But I can tell you that at least two people I know who invested with J&D are now dead."

Brenda pressed a hand to her mouth. Dear God, this was real. There was no option for coincidence and no accidental or maybe even natural events to blame.

"Mr. Holland," Ben said, "my agency was hired to protect Ms. Devers and her daughter and to try and figure out what's going on here. Any insights you are willing to share could be immensely helpful."

"I can't help you because I only know two things. I have five million dollars missing and people are dropping like flies. Go into hiding, Ms. Devers, and let someone else figure this out. I suspect it's way, way over our heads."

"Thank you, Mr. Holland," Ben said. He held up a business card in view of the camera. "This is my contact information. If you recall anything you want to pass along please call me."

The man said nothing further.

Brenda walked alongside Ben as they retraced their steps to his car. Since they had been in view of the car the entire time there was no need to check it for trouble. She settled into the passenger seat and waited for Ben to get behind the wheel.

"What do we do now?" She was so tired of dead ends. They so desperately needed a break.

"Now we're going back to your place. Have some lunch

and check in with my colleague to see where he is with his research."

She collapsed against the headrest and watched the landscape go by. She wondered if Tate's wife knew about any of this. Probably not. Brenda certainly had not. Then again, she and Scott had lived separately for a year. Maybe she'd missed all the dirty details because of that. She should just go to the woman's house and demand to know whatever she knew. Except she had a big-deal lawyer.

Her cell phone rang, and Brenda dug it from her handbag. Maybe it was Mallory. Brenda had called this morning to talk to Janey, but the call had gone to voicemail. She checked the screen. Not Mallory or one of Brenda's contacts, but she recognized the number.

"It's Detective Shelton."

"Cummings has likely told him about our trespassing on a crime scene last evening."

With a sigh of dread, she accepted the call. "Brenda Devers."

"Ms. Devers," the detective said, "can you come to my office? We've found the intruder who broke into your home, and he won't answer any of our questions. He says he will talk only to you. I realize this request is unusual, but we could really use your help."

Stunned but definitely game for the opportunity, she assured him, "We'll be there in ten minutes."

The detective thanked her and ended the call.

"You're never going to believe this."

Ben shot her a look. "Try me."

"Shelton says they have the intruder in custody, but he won't talk to anyone but me." They had just turned onto her street.

Ben laughed, a dry sound. "Point me in the right direction."

Evidently Scott had not been the intruder…but even if this suspect confessed, could she really trust his words were true?

Huntsville Police Department
Wheeler Avenue
Huntsville, 1:00 p.m.

BRENDA WASN'T SURE what she had expected, but the man secured in the interview room wasn't it. She stood in the observation booth, staring through the glass at him, wondering why he would possibly want to talk to her.

According to his driver's license, the intruder was Dirk Lanier, thirty-five, of Birmingham. His prints weren't in any database and the driver's license was apparently a fake—there was no way to confirm anything about him. Ben called him a ghost.

Lanier sat at a table in the center of the beige room. He looked to be of medium height and build. Muscular. His head was shaven clean, but his jaw sported a five-o'clock shadow. He stared steadily at the glass as if he could see those watching him, but that wasn't how it worked.

Brenda and Ben had been escorted to the observation booth by Detective Shelton. Another detective, Reginald Truss, had joined them.

"Because he insists on speaking to you privately," Shelton said, "he agreed to be secured. We didn't want you going in there otherwise. His hands are cuffed behind his back, and we have shackles on his ankles that are secured to the floor. That's why we had to use this room. It's the only one outfitted for that sort of thing."

Brenda nodded. "Okay."

"Do not get close to him," Truss cautioned, picking up from there. "Walk through the door and sit down on this side of the table. If he gives you any lip, just get up and walk right back out. He's already admitted to being the one who came into your home. He just refuses to tell us why or who sent him. He will only talk to you about that."

"Okay," Brenda repeated. She wanted to get in there and see what the man had to say. If there was any chance he could tell them something more…she was game.

Shelton opened the door to lead her from the booth. Ben gave her a nod. "I'll be watching," he promised.

She managed a smile. No matter how ready she was to do this, she was still nervous. Damned nervous. She told herself that if this intruder had wanted to really hurt her he could have when he was in her house. Maybe he'd been ordered to do no harm since the people who hired him wanted something from her.

Trouble was, she had no idea what they wanted or where it was.

Just outside the door that exited the booth was the door that led into the interview room. Shelton opened it and said to the man seated inside, "You've got five minutes. Pull any crap and you'll wish you hadn't."

The man, Dirk Lanier, said nothing. He never even looked at Shelton. He just stared at Brenda. She figured it was a mind game. He wanted her scared.

Well, he'd succeeded…a little. But she wasn't about to show him just how much.

She did as Shelton had instructed. She walked to the vacant chair on her side of the table, pulled it out and sat down. She stared directly at the man across the table and waited.

No need to attempt small talk. She wasn't even sure how that was done with a man like this.

"Your husband left you in a world of hurt, lady."

"Well, he never was a very good husband." She held her hands together in her lap, twisting them now as her nerves started to jangle.

"Not much of a daddy either," the man added with a sneer.

Brenda said nothing. What was the point?

"If you—" he lowered his voice to barely a whisper "—want that little girl of yours to be safe, there's something you should know."

Heart pounding harder, Brenda leaned slightly forward to ensure she didn't miss what he said next. "I'm listening."

He did the same, but his move put their noses so close that his would have touched hers had she not drawn back slightly. No small amount of fear crowded into her throat. She struggled to ignore it. To pay attention to how he smelled…to the color of his eyes. Hazel with a distinct hint of silver. Was he the intruder who had pushed her into the wall? She couldn't say. She forced herself to take another deep breath. Sweaty flesh was the only scent she detected.

"You better listen good," he murmured, "because I'm only going to say this once."

She nodded stiffly.

"And—" he narrowed his eyes at her "—if you tell the cops what I say, you'll be sorry."

Chapter Fifteen

1:40 p.m.

"What the hell is he saying?" Shelton demanded.

Ben stared at the scene playing out on the other side of the glass. Tension rifled through him, and the urge to bust into that interview room was a living, breathing need growing inside him. But he held back… If this man had information they needed, he couldn't do anything to stop the momentum.

Suddenly, Brenda stood and walked away from the table.

Shelton had already exited the observation booth and, as soon as she opened the interview room door, was demanding to know what happened. Brenda appeared visibly shaken. Ben pushed his way between the two detectives and went to her side.

"You okay?"

She nodded. "He said—" she surveyed the two detectives "—that you're never going to find the truth."

"What the hell does that mean?" Shelton demanded.

Truss went into the interview room and started to rant at the man shackled inside.

"I don't know," Brenda insisted. "I can only assume this whole thing is some sort of bizarre game. They've been playing games from the beginning."

"Who has been playing games?" Shelton roared.

Ben shut the door to the interview room with his foot and pointed a glower at the man. "You, for one. You and Agent Cummings both. Brenda has been lied to—"

"I have not lied," Shelton argued, clearly outraged.

Good. It was about time, in Ben's opinion, that someone besides Brenda was on the receiving end of all the doubt and accusations.

"Maybe only by omission," Ben allowed, "but you have not been truthful with us, and this is enough. Brenda will no longer cooperate with your investigation if you're going to leave her in the dark this way. It's dangerous, primarily to her. Or maybe you haven't noticed."

Shelton held up his hands. "We're doing all we can."

"What about her car? Anything back from the lab? Do you have any results back on *anything*?" Ben demanded. "Where are you and Cummings on the investigation into the firm? Is it true that money belonging to several clients is missing? Have you done anything at all in the effort to find Scott Devers, who—by your own admission—is still alive?"

Shelton opened his mouth to respond but then he frowned. He dug into the pocket of his rumpled jacket and retrieved his cell phone. "Shelton," he barked to the caller.

Ben turned to Brenda, who was still standing there looking ready to run. The man in that room had told her something—something she had not shared with Shelton. Ben needed to get her out of here to learn what he'd said. He also wanted to touch base with Chicago to see if there was anything back on their series of numbers.

Shelton swore and ended the call. He opened the door to the interview room. "Take him back to holding. His lawyer is signing in."

"Can we go now?" Brenda asked, obviously wanting out of this corridor before Lanier was brought out of the room.

Shelton glared at her again. "If you think of something more he said, I'm sure you'll let me know."

"He didn't say anything else."

Ben put a hand at the small of her back and ushered her away from the detective. As they walked away, he heard Shelton ask Lanier, "How the hell did a guy like you afford an attorney like Carlisle?"

If Lanier opted to answer, they were out of earshot. The sooner Ben got Brenda out of here the better.

When the rental car had been checked and they were inside, buckled up and driving away, she said, "I lied to Detective Shelton."

Ben glanced at her. "Do you want to tell me why?"

She exhaled a big breath and stared out the car window. "He said if I told the cops I would be sorry. So I didn't."

"In that case I wouldn't have told them either." Unless his message contained some revelation about an impending murder or attack of some sort, she wasn't obliged to share the contents of a personal conversation with anyone.

"He said Scott is dead." She stared forward then. "Then he warned that if I didn't find what they needed within twenty-four hours that Janey would..." She closed her eyes.

Ben reached for her hand. "We're not going to let them get to Janey."

She shook her head. "How can we stop them?" She turned to look at him. "Really, how can we possibly assume the idea is even possible? This is a huge cartel. I did some googling about them, and you're right, they are ruthless. Worse than any of the others. And there are literally hundreds if not thousands of them operating all over the place. Unless I find what they want, how can I hope to keep out of their reach—much less stop them?"

There was no arguing her conclusions. The upside was that she and her daughter would be dead already if the cartel wanted them that way. Obviously there was something else they wanted. Something that required allowing her to live long enough to find it. The downside was that even if the cartel got whatever it was they wanted, that didn't ensure Brenda's or Janey's safety.

"We will do whatever necessary," he promised.

He didn't want to bring up the idea of witness protection. The agency had its own program to help those who needed to disappear. He hoped that wouldn't prove necessary for Brenda and her daughter, but at this point he couldn't make promises beyond the one he'd just made.

"I feel like I should cry if what he said is true, that Scott is dead." She sighed. "But I think I may have cried all the tears I had for him. The truth is I've cried for him so many times that it seems ridiculous to cry again. I cried so much with Janey after the explosion. I swear there are just no more tears for him left in me." She shook her head. "None. Do I sound awful?"

"You sound—" he looked to her for a moment then settled his attention back on the street "—like someone who has been pushed to her limit. Trust me, anyone else would have reached that place long ago. You have been more than sufficiently forgiving and incredibly decent about all of this. Not only did he cheat multiple times, but he left you holding this enormous bag of trouble. I would throw in that he has shown no care for your or Janey's safety if not for the fact that he reached out to the Colby Agency."

"That was probably just to keep from feeling guilty," she protested.

Ben had to laugh. She was mentally exhausted and not about to give the man an inch. "I'm taking you to lunch. Pick the spot."

"Food…? I'm not sure I care." She gasped and turned to Ben. "I just realized something that might be important. Did you hear that detective say that Lanier had a big-deal attorney signing in?"

"I did. Do you know the attorney?"

"Only by name." A realization dawned in her expression. "Oh my God. Carlisle is the attorney Lena Jenner hired. How's that for a coincidence?"

Ben would bet just about anything it wasn't a coincidence at all. "We may need to pay an impromptu visit to Ms. Jenner."

"Definitely," Brenda agreed.

The same car that had made every turn he had since leaving the police department popped up in his rearview mirror once more. Silver sedan. Blond driver. Sunglasses.

Well, damn.

"Hang on. We have a tail."

Chapter Sixteen

2:00 p.m.

"Is it the same sedan that followed us before?" Brenda resisted the impulse to turn around and stare out the rear window. Her pulse rate had already jumped into a frantic mode.

Every time they took what felt like a half step forward, something else happened to drag them back two steps.

Or maybe they hadn't moved forward at all.

"Different color," Ben points out. "The other one was black and there's also a different driver."

"Do we just keep driving or go home or turn around and go back to the police department?" This was so exasperating. When would they get to a point where they felt like they were moving forward?

Never, it seemed.

This Lanier person—the intruder, if he hadn't lied about that too—was the perfect example. Brenda had arrived at the interview in hopes he had something to tell her that would help her understand how to stop this nightmare. But he'd done nothing but warn her of the consequences if she didn't resolve it.

How was she supposed to know what to do?

Maybe the only way out of this was to take Janey and

run. They could hide and hope they were never found. If Scott was really dead…

Except she had no idea what the truth was anymore, and the cartel's resources were far too powerful, too broad to make running away so simple.

Obviously there was no winning against these people. The best she could hope for was to give them whatever it was they wanted and pray they went away. If she hadn't been so depressed she would have laughed out loud at the thought.

Ben made a sudden right turn and braked to a stop. Brenda looked around at the closed food market and the abandoned parking lot. Why had they stopped? She turned to Ben. She reminded herself that he was a professional. He knew what he was doing.

"When I get out of the car, lock the doors. Climb over the console, and if there's trouble drive away as fast as you can."

"What? No way. I'm not—"

"Do it." He opened his door and emerged from the car.

Brenda hit the lock button and scrambled into the driver's seat. She twisted around to stare out the rear window. The air refused to fill her lungs and her heart thundered so hard she was certain it would burst any moment. If something happened to him, what would she and Janey do? Plus…she really liked him. Really, really liked him.

Please don't get yourself killed.

The driver's-side door of the other vehicle opened. Brenda's world seemed to decelerate into slow motion, yet somehow the fear and anticipation kept building at a rapid-fire pace.

Please don't let this guy have a gun.

Blond hair. Sunglasses.

Not a man. Brenda drew back a little. It was a woman.

The driver closed her door, leaned against it and removed

her sunglasses. Recognition slammed into Brenda. This was the woman from LAX. The one with Scott on Tuesday.

Brenda was out of the car before she had time to think through the step. She left the door wide open and stormed toward Ben and the other woman. By God, she would have answers from this woman.

"It's her," she shouted to Ben. "She's the woman from the airport. The one I saw with Scott on Tuesday."

A whole other stunning reality hit Brenda then. It had only been two days. *Two days.* Forty-eight hours since all hell broke loose in her and Janey's lives. Since her world changed for the second time in less than a month. She wilted. Grabbed on to the front of the woman's car for support.

"Who are you?" she demanded.

Ben was already speaking to this person, but Brenda didn't care. She needed to understand how this all happened. How this woman was connected to Scott. And why all of this—this total insanity—was happening.

"I don't have a lot of time," the blonde said to Brenda. "I've been trying to get a message to you since Tuesday night."

"Who are you?" Brenda repeated, beyond angry now.

"I used to work for Scott," she said. "I was once a court reporter until I got burned out. But I'm still a really good transcriptionist. I've worked for medical practices, law firms. All sorts of places. For Scott, I would transcribe his conference calls and even the face-to-face meetings. He recorded everything. He would send the recordings to me, and I would enter the dialogue into a program. A quick edit and then I'd drop the typed pages into this file hosting service where he would retrieve them."

Sounded exactly like something Scott would want to do with his client meetings. Still, Brenda would just bet their relationship had not been a working one only. This woman, whoever she was, was exactly his type. Tall, thin and blonde. And gorgeous.

"I missed your name," Ben said.

He hadn't missed it; she was yet to give it. Brenda silently steamed.

"Ginger York. I live in New Hope but most of my clients are here in Huntsville."

"Why were you in Los Angeles with him?" Brenda wanted to hear this. *Transcribing a meeting for a man who was supposed to be dead?*

"He was asked to go to Los Angeles by a man he thought could help him with the trouble he'd gotten into. He asked me to go with him so that we looked like a couple traveling. He hoped people would look at me instead of him." She rolled her eyes. "That's why I was wearing that racy dress. I wouldn't usually wear something so daring during daylight."

As furious as Brenda was, the story sort of made sense. "Did it not cross your mind that he was supposed to be dead?"

"Hell yeah! He almost scared me to death when he showed up at my place." She pressed a hand to her chest as if her heart were running away just recalling the event. "I mean, I live in the middle of nowhere. In a cabin—sort of off the grid. I don't get many visitors unless it's someone I've invited. And, as you say, I thought he was dead. It was freaky for sure."

"How did he explain his resurrection?" Ben asked.

Brenda might have laughed at the question if she hadn't been so outraged. This woman made it seem totally not a big deal that a man she thought blew up in his office showed up at her house—other than it was a little startling.

"He said he had a bad feeling about the meeting—the one

at his office the day of the explosion, I mean. His handler from the FBI, Chris or Clint, I can't remember his name, had called an emergency meeting."

"You knew he was working with the FBI?" Brenda was fairly sure that her blood pressure was going to make her brain explode.

"I did not," Ginger insisted. "I'm just telling you what he told me. That surprised me too. Anyway, there was this guy with him that day. Some guy from the cartel—can you believe that? Poor Scott was involved with a freaking drug cartel. He said it was Jenner's idea."

Of course he did, Brenda mused. Poor Scott was never the cause of problems.

"Anyway," she went on, "he didn't want to go to the office because he knew his handler would be there and this cartel guy wouldn't go away. But then the cartel guy demanded to see Tate, and Tate was at the office with the handler guy, who was pretending to be a new big-deal client."

"Did he mention the name of the man from the cartel?" Ben asked.

Ginger shook her head. "I don't think so, but honestly the story was so out there, and I was so shocked, I may not be remembering everything."

"How did he get out before the explosion?" Brenda was ready for her to speed up the storytelling and get to the important parts.

"He said when they arrived at the office, the cartel guy saw the FBI guy and everything went crazy. Scott saw an opportunity in the middle of the fray to slip out." Her eyes got bigger with every word. "So he rushed out the back door. He said he barely got out of the building before it exploded."

"What about his partner?" Brenda demanded, appalled. "Did he not try to save him?" Given this new twist about the attorney, Brenda wasn't sure she should have any sympathy for Tate Jenner. His wife was using the same attorney as the cartel. Since Carlisle had this impressive reputation, she supposed it could be coincidence. But no way was she automatically giving the woman that kind of grace.

"He didn't because he was already dead," Ginger told her. "The cartel guy shot Tate. Then he was grilling the FBI guy, which is the only reason Scott had a chance to run. The cartel guy shot at him when he ran, but Scott figured he wasn't trying for a lethal shot since he was the only one left who knew all the accounts and passwords."

Brenda shared a look with Ben. So maybe those numbers on the paper they had found were account numbers. But what about the passwords?

"You're sure Scott said his partner was shot?" Ben pressed.

"Oh yeah. Scared the heck out of Scott. He knew he had to get out of there and that he couldn't let them catch him under any circumstances."

Even if it meant throwing his wife and child under the bus, Brenda mused. Another wave of fury washed over her—at the police as well as at Scott. She wanted to call Shelton and demand to know why he hadn't mentioned the shooting to her. Because he had lied to her. Shelton had kept that from her, and God only knew what else.

"Do you know where Scott is now?" Brenda wanted to find him and punch him for leaving them in this horrific mess.

"No. That's the weird part. I've called him over and over, and I've gone by all the places I could think of that he might go and he's nowhere."

And just like that they still had nothing. Nothing!

"About these recordings," Ben said. "Did Scott record all his meetings?"

"Most, I think, but I can't be sure of course."

"Do you have access to the sessions you transcribed for him?"

"No. Once I dropped the documents into the hosting site, I deleted them. And my only access to the site is to drop off. I can't retrieve anything."

"Do you recall the name of the host site?"

"Sure. It's YourBox."

"Thank you. Any particular reason you were following us today?" Ben asked.

Brenda leaned a hip against the front fender. She would like to know the answer to that one as well. This whole thing was like a bad movie. Why hadn't Scott come forward? If he really wanted to protect her and Janey, why not work with the police to stop this whole thing?

Because, she understood, he was only really concerned about protecting himself. She and Janey were afterthoughts. She glanced at Ben. Not that the Colby Agency could ever be considered anything but an amazing option. Still, it was the idea that Scott had waited until he was eyeball deep in trouble to consider his child and her mother.

"He gave me a message for you." She turned to Brenda as she said this. "I came to your house Tuesday night to bring it to you, but someone was watching the house and I freaked. Then I came by Wednesday morning and there were cops everywhere. So I just went home and hid. But then I got to thinking about how Scott made me promise that I would see that you got the message, so I came to your house again today, but you were driving away. This time I followed you. When I saw you turn into the police department, I just waited. I knew you'd come out eventually."

"What's the message?" Brenda was ready to get this over with. Clearly this woman knew no more than they did about the cartel.

"Oh yeah." Ginger poked her head back into the car and drew back with an envelope. She handed it to Brenda. "Scott sort of freaked out when he saw you at the airport. He was worried he was being watched, and, if he was, he thought they might think you were meeting him there. That's why we gave you the slip. It wasn't because he didn't want to see you."

Maybe she shouldn't, but the explanation made Brenda feel a little better about that awful moment. "Thank you."

Ginger surveyed the street. "I should get out of here." She looked to Brenda again. "Good luck. I hope you guys figure all this out and no one else gets hurt."

With that, she climbed into her car and drove away.

Brenda stared at the envelope where her name was written in bold strokes. It was Scott's handwriting for sure.

"Let's get in the car and get to your house," Ben suggested.

She waited until she was in the car and Ben had pulled out onto the street, then she opened the envelope. It was a handwritten note.

No matter that she and Scott had not been together for so long, a sadness swelled inside her. Dirk Lanier had told her Scott was dead…for real this time. But Ginger didn't seem to know it. Who knew?

Brenda,

I know this is all crazy right now, but I swear to you I tried to handle it. I wanted to protect you and Janey from this. Unfortunately, that proved impossible.

When I was in real trouble and there was no way out, I called the Colby Agency.

Someone from the agency should be there with you by now. You can trust them implicitly. But *do not* trust anyone else. No one. Please trust *no one*. Take Janey and go hide somewhere safe. The Colby Agency can help with that. I will get this straightened out, you have my word. I know my word doesn't mean much to you anymore, but I swear to you I will fix this. Right now, I just need the two of you to stay safe. I will always love you both.

Scott

Brenda squeezed her eyes shut to stop the damned tears. She had thought she was out of tears for Scott. For that matter she couldn't be sure that man—Dirk Lanier—was telling her the truth. Scott could still be alive for all she knew. This whole thing could be a trick.

Either way, she had to protect Janey, and to do that she had to protect herself. She was all Janey had left.

She called Mallory. Brenda tried to slow her respiration as she waited through ring after ring. The call went to voicemail. She waited a whole minute and called again. Same ring, ring, ring and then voicemail.

"I can't get Mallory to answer," she said, the pitch of her voice rising with each word. "I left her a message this morning, but she hasn't called me back."

Ben braked for a red traffic light. "Take a breath and tell me what the letter said."

She closed her eyes and struggled with the mounting panic. "He told me how sorry he was and how he'd called your agency. But the really important part is that he said I should not trust anyone but you and your agency. No one else. Now I'm worried that I shouldn't have trusted Mallory. I've always been able to trust her, but with all that's happened..."

Her heart raced harder. She couldn't catch a full breath.

"Okay." The light changed, and he accelerated away from the intersection. "Does Mallory have any family here?"

"Yes, her mother and father."

"Call whichever one you can reach and see if they've heard from her."

"Okay. Good idea." She should have thought of that. A quick scroll through her contacts and she found Mrs. Lawrence's number. She placed the call, then waited through first one, then two, then a third ring. The call went to voicemail. The panic surged once more. "No answer."

"What's her address?" he asked. "Some people don't keep their cell phones handy all the time."

Brenda recited the address, then tried the number again. Still no answer.

"Does she have a house phone?"

Brenda shook her head. "I don't know." Her heart ached with each rapid thud against her breastbone.

Thankfully Mrs. Lawrence lived on the Oakwood side of Five Points, so it didn't take long to reach her house. A car in the driveway gave Brenda hope there was someone home. Ben was likely right. Mrs. Lawrence might not keep her phone attached to her the way Brenda did.

She and Ben got out together and walked to the door. While Ben knocked—there was no doorbell—Brenda peeked through a front window. Couldn't help herself. She was worried sick.

Charlene Lawrence sat in her recliner, mouth open, eyes closed. Fear shot through Brenda like a spear. "Oh my God, she looks dead."

Ben leaned over and had a look through the window. "I think I see—"

The older woman's eyes suddenly opened, and her mouth closed. Brenda almost fainted with relief. Ben reached over and rapped on the door again.

When it opened, Mrs. Lawrence looked from Brenda to Ben and back. "Hello." She drew the door open wider. "Come in. Sorry if you've been knocking awhile. I was taking a little nap."

"I don't want to disturb you, Mrs. Lawrence," Brenda said. "I was wondering if you had heard from Mallory."

The woman made a face of severe concentration. "No, I don't think so. You know she's always busy working. For you." She smiled big and bright. "I just love when she brings Janey by for a visit. Such a sweet child."

Brenda managed a stiff nod. "Have you heard from her since she and Janey went up to the cabin?"

Mrs. Lawrence made a new face then, this one confused or uncertain. "I think there must be some miscommunication, hon. None of us ever seemed to have the time to go anymore, so we sold the cabin last spring. She couldn't be there."

Something different rushed through Brenda then. Bigger than plain old fear…colder, thicker. *Sheer terror.* "She told me she was taking Janey to the cabin." Brenda forced her tone to remain calm despite the hysteria attempting to take hold deep inside her. "Is there someplace else she might have meant?"

"No." Mrs. Lawrence shook her head. "I can't think of any place offhand. She would have told me if she was going out of town. Did you try Peter? Maybe she's at his house." Her smile returned. "He'll know where she is. I'm sure of it."

"Thank you, Mrs. Lawrence," Brenda managed to say

without falling apart. "If you hear from Mallory please ask her to call me."

"I sure will, hon. I hope you're holding up okay," she offered. "Mallory said your husband's death has been just awful for you."

Brenda thanked her and then she and Ben rushed away. The idea that her child was missing started to arrow its way into her chest. *No, please no.*

She told herself Mrs. Lawrence was right. Peter would know…but he was supposed to be with them.

When they were in the car after the usual check that took forever it felt like to Brenda, Ben said, "Where does this Peter live?"

"He has an apartment downtown, but he should be with Mallory." Hands shaking, she dug out her cell once more. "I have his number." *Please, please let him answer.*

Peter picked up on the first ring. "Hey, Brenda."

Thank God. "Hey, Peter. I need to speak with Mallory. It's really important." Brenda held tightly to the phone, her mind whirling with worry and fear and hope and other things she didn't want to name.

"Ah, sorry, Brenda, but she's not with me. Maybe Mallory didn't tell you, but she and I broke up."

Oh God. No. "Really?" Brenda glanced at Ben, desperately clinging to the ability to hold herself together. "I'm so sorry. When did this happen?"

"Not quite a month ago. She just up and told me one day that we were done. It was a shock, let me tell you. I'd already bought an engagement ring to give her at Christmas. I'm still trying to figure it out."

"I'm so sorry, Peter." *Hang on… Don't lose it.* "I asked her to take Janey out of town for a couple of days since all this business with Scott has started up again. I thought she said she was going to the cabin. But her mom says they sold the cabin. Do you have any idea where she might have gone instead? She's not answering today, and I'm a little nervous."

"I don't know, Brenda. I mean, gosh, that's kind of crazy. Maybe she was going through something. I will say that back when we were together—near the end—I got this whole thing in my head that she and Scott were having an affair. Anyway, I don't know. Whatever is going on, I'm sorry I can't help you."

"I… Thank you, Peter. Please tell her to call me if you hear from her."

"'Course I will, but I'm not expecting to hear from her."

"Right. Okay. Thanks, Peter."

Brenda ended the call. "They broke up." She turned to Ben. "He thought she was having an affair with Scott, but I don't think so." She drew in a big breath. "Honestly, at this point I don't know anything. Except…" She swallowed at the tightening in her throat. "My daughter is missing and I'm terrified."

"We're going back to Shelton's office to file a missing person report," he assured her. "We may or may not be able to trust him, but we need people on the lookout. There are steps that need to be taken that only the police can take. Now. Right now."

He was right. Brenda sank back into her seat. Here she'd thought this nightmare couldn't get any worse. But she had been so very wrong.

Her child was missing.

Chapter Seventeen

Huntsville Police Department
Wheeler Avenue
Huntsville, 3:30 p.m.

Ben sat next to Brenda as she explained all she had learned this afternoon about Mallory Lawrence and how she had not been able to contact her since around eight last night, and even then she had not been able to speak with her daughter.

"But," Detective Shelton said, "you asked Ms. Lawrence to take your child and hide out. Isn't that correct?"

Ben wanted to punch the man, and if it were not for being arrested and separated from Brenda he would. Damn it. But he couldn't risk allowing her out of his sight with all that was happening. The situation had escalated to the worst possible scenario.

"That's correct," Ben answered for Brenda when she only stared at the detective. "But there were specific instructions attached. Now we've learned that Ms. Lawrence lied about being able to take the child where she told Brenda she was taking her. Ms. Lawrence's own mother has not heard from her in days. Not to mention, Ms. Lawrence specifically said that her boyfriend was going with them to the cabin. As it turns out, she dumped her boyfriend a month ago."

"Maybe she has a new boyfriend," Shelton tossed back.

The man was trying Ben's patience in the worst way. "Regardless," he argued, "Ms. Lawrence clearly had an agenda not known to Brenda. Now Janey is missing. I'm confident we both understand the law and the proper procedures for this sort of situation with a vulnerable minor child."

Shelton eyed him for a moment. "We do, yes. Well." He turned to Brenda. "Let's get that paperwork done, shall we?"

Ben's cell vibrated. He leaned toward Brenda. "I have to take a call. I'll be right outside the office if you need me." He looked to Shelton then. "I'm sure the detective has everything in hand to take the necessary steps."

As much as he hated leaving her for even a moment, he stepped out of the office but stayed close. Brenda was beside herself with fear for her child, and she had every right to be. This was an increasingly dangerous situation.

He drew out his phone and accepted the call from his colleague. He'd hoped to hear from him today. Brenda was swiftly running out of hope. "What do you have for me, Max?" he asked. "Something that will help us crack this one, I hope."

"Maybe not anything that significant," Max allowed. "But perhaps a little something to help you along. The numbers you provided are definitely account numbers. We've narrowed them down to the bank—which was not readily discernible since the first part of the numbers were actually the routing numbers, but they were written in a pattern that had to be deciphered. It took a minute."

Ben had anticipated there was an issue with the numbers, but he had known Max was the man for the job. "Are the accounts listed under either Scott Devers or Tate Jenner?"

"Actually," Max explained, "they're listed under the name Brenda Devers."

That was something Ben hadn't seen coming. "That would mean only Brenda Devers could access them."

"More or less," Max agreed. "Anyone who presented with the proper identification as Brenda Devers and who knew the account numbers as well as the passcodes could access whatever funds the accounts contain."

"Did you find anything else on Mallory Lawrence?"

"I have a list of former addresses and employers. I forwarded those to your email along with the rest of my findings. I am digging deeper for any addresses that might still be active under her name. As far as any criminal record, there isn't one under that name or involving those fingerprints."

That was possibly a good thing. "Anything new on the cartel's activities in the Huntsville area? I sent you the name Dirk Lanier. He had a fake driver's license that listed him as being from Birmingham."

"There's nothing on the name Dirk Lanier. But I tapped into the database the Huntsville Police Department used for running his prints. As the detective told you, there is nothing in the database, but I also ran him through Interpol. I'm not sure why the detective didn't do the same since Lanier is suspected of being associated with a South American drug cartel. The good news—or bad depending on how you look at it—is that I got a hit at Interpol. As you suspected, the alleged intruder, Dirk Lanier, is an alias for a known cartel assassin. Interpol should be contacting the detective about him as well as about the unidentified victim from the explosion. His DNA results had not been sent to Interpol until I *borrowed* them and sent them along. The guy is cartel as well."

The information about Lanier and the other explosion victim confirmed what York had told them. The cartel was aware that Brenda might be the key to getting whatever it was that Devers had taken from them—most likely money. Otherwise, Lanier would have killed her and Janey the night he entered their home. In Ben's opinion, these details also confirmed that Lanier was likely the intruder. Even the address left under the Barbie elevator was obviously part of the game. Had Scott Devers suggested the man use a hiding place like that to ensure Brenda found it? Probably not. Ben had a feeling Devers was staying far away from anyone related to the cartel. More likely, Lanier was one who did his homework and drew his own conclusions.

"Anything else?" Ben was grateful for the information. It was far more than they had gotten from the detective or the Bureau. Even tying up one or two loose ends was useful in an investigation like this one.

"The special agent you mentioned… Cummings."

"Yes. Did you find something relevant on him?"

"Nope. That's the problem. He doesn't exist."

Well, now, that would certainly explain the aura of deceit Ben had picked up on in the man's presence. "Do you have any specifics at all?"

"Since I don't have his fingerprints, I ran that pic you snapped by a friend at Interpol. He says this guy is some high-up mucky-muck involved with the cartel. We can't confirm this, of course, without prints. But he was pretty sure based on the photo. If someone that far up the food chain is there, watching your client and pretending to be a part of the investigation, then this is big. Really big. I sent you what I learned on him—assuming he's the man my contact thinks he is. If he is, that would explain why nothing related to the investigation is reaching Interpol."

"Thanks, Max. I'll get back to you. If I find a way to get Cummings's prints I'll shoot them your way."

"You got it."

"Wait." Ben had been mulling over the partner, Tate Jenner. "See if you can find anything else on Tate Jenner and his wife, Lena. With all that's happened seemingly connecting Brenda to what Scott was doing, let's see if the same was being done with Jenner's wife." Then he gave his colleague a quick update on the news from Ginger York, the blonde from LAX.

"Thanks for the update," Max said. "I'll call when I have something."

The call ended. This was all good information, but none of it was good news. Brenda was in way, way over her head here. So was Detective Shelton for that matter. His investigation was going nowhere because he was trusting Cummings to coordinate between local PD and places like Interpol.

Bottom line, Scott Devers had screwed up royally. Either that or he'd built a multilayered cover to hide what he was really doing. Had Tate been killed to take him out of play… so all was forfeited to Scott? That scenario was suddenly gaining momentum for Ben. Once he had something more to go on, he would move in that direction.

He rapped on the detective's door before entering his office. Brenda was just signing the necessary paperwork. Good timing.

"We'll get the Amber Alert going," Shelton assured her. "As soon as we hear anything at all you'll know."

Ben made a curious face. "I haven't seen your friend Agent Cummings around today. Should we be worried he's disappeared as well?"

Shelton got to his feet, following Brenda's lead. "Got no idea. The feds do what the feds do. You should know that."

No question. "We all set?" Ben looked to Brenda.

She nodded. "I really need to go home right now."

"Of course." As they reached the door, Ben paused and

glanced back at Shelton. "We're counting on you to help us find Janey."

Shelton nodded. "I'm on it."

"Maybe," Ben suggested, "you should check in with Agent Cummings's superior. There's something about him." Ben shook his head. "I'm not sure he's got your back, Shelton."

The detective said nothing. When it all came out, he wouldn't be able to say Ben hadn't warned him.

The worst part about this case, Ben concluded, as they made their way out of the building, was the fact that so far they had found no one at all they dared to trust. Evidently Scott Devers was correct in warning his wife not to trust anyone.

Outside he went through the usual routine before they climbed into the car. It was tedious but unfortunately necessary.

"Did your colleague give you any news?" Brenda asked as they drove away from the police department.

"When we get to your house we'll go over the details in the email Max sent me."

"Then," she said, staring at his profile, "I'm going out to find my daughter and I'm not going to stop until I do."

"We'll do it together," he agreed.

He wouldn't sleep again until he found her.

Chapter Eighteen

Devers Residence
White Street
Huntsville, 5:30 p.m.

The Amber Alert had been issued. The idea that her child was the missing child involved ripped her insides to shreds.

As difficult as it was, Brenda had to focus. To that end, she sat on a stool at the island and reviewed with Ben the information his colleague had sent. She had reached that place—the one where numbness and an overwhelming sense of disbelief had taken over. Her emotions were still there but they were impotent against the other…the unfeeling emptiness.

"Should we call Detective Shelton about what your friend found on Cummings?" At this point she was so far past expecting good news that she felt on the verge of a breakdown. She needed to find her child. This was her fault… She was the one who sent her away with Mallory. She should have kept her right here with her.

Her lips trembled, and she fought to hang on to the last vestiges of her composure.

All she wanted in this world was her child back. Safe and happy…the way she'd been the other night playing Barbie dolls.

Brenda had been a fool twice over—first with her husband and then with Mallory.

"I'm not sure that would be the right move," Ben said.

His response surprised her, pulled her away from that awful, awful haunted place she'd fallen into. "Why?" That she managed the word without her voice trembling was a miracle.

"The way Shelton has dragged his feet and withheld information," he explained, his eyes searching hers as if he understood how she felt without her having to say the words out loud, "I'm concerned that we may not be able to trust him completely. Better to wait on that one. I gave him a warning. We'll see if he follows through. Either way, his actions won't lead back to you."

The point was a valid one. Frankly, she wasn't sure it was possible to trust anyone other than this man next to her.

He touched her arm, just the briefest brush of his fingers. "I won't ask if you're okay. I know you're not. But I want you to understand that I will find her. I want you to believe that."

She nodded, barely restraining the tears. Damn it. She hated all the crying. *Deep breath.* "What if I call Agent Cummings? I have his number. I could tell him that I have what the cartel is looking for—I believe—and I'd like to turn it over to him. I can say I don't trust Detective Shelton and I felt I needed to come directly to him since he's with the FBI."

She recognized from the look on Ben's face that he didn't see it as a particularly good idea. But she was desperate. She had to find her daughter. And as much as she trusted him, Lanier's warning that she only had twenty-four hours had come just before she learned Janey and Mallory were missing. That had to mean something. And time was running out.

"I know it's a risk," she said before he could tell her all the reasons it was a potential mistake. "But Lanier warned me that I had twenty-four hours. I'm sure the clock started when he issued that warning. At the time I didn't realize his people might already have Janey. But they must have her. Or at least someone on their payroll. Why else would Mallory be missing with her? Somehow she's either involved with this and they're using Janey as leverage or she's a victim too." Fear rammed through the numbness that had shrouded her. "Either way, we have to find her, and as much as I trust you to do exactly what you say, I need to be doing something too."

"All right." Ben gave her a nod. "We'll set it in motion, but we have to plan carefully and strategically."

"You're in charge of planning," she relented. "I'm too emotionally gutted."

"I'm glad you recognize the disadvantage. It's a very difficult time, and I don't envy you the next few hours and days. But I will do all within my power to get this done quickly."

She really was lucky that Scott had called the Colby Agency. She wasn't sure how she would have survived this without Ben's help. She refocused on the matter at hand. As easy as it would be to allow her mind to escape the pressure by getting caught up in thoughts about their night together, she couldn't do that right now. Finding her little girl was all that mattered. No deviating from that singular goal, no matter how badly she needed to find just one moment of peace.

"You call him," Ben instructed, "and tell him you believe you've found something important. Ask for a meeting as quickly as possible. Preferably we would want him to come here, but if he insists on someplace else, we'll have to figure out how we're going to handle the logistics. We'll deal with that possibility if the need arises."

"Okay." Anticipation started to chase away all those other choking feelings. "Do I describe to Cummings what I've found? He may ask what it is. Where I found it."

"Tell him it's a series of names and numbers you found hidden in your house. But nothing more. Even if he presses the issue, do not give him anything over the phone."

"Right. Got it."

"It's six now," Ben went on. "See if he'll agree to meet at seven. If he really wants what you've found, he'll agree. An hour will give him plenty of time to make calls and drive here. We'll be ready for him." He smiled. "I'll set up a video camera, and I'll be armed."

A frown drew her lips downward. "You carry a weapon?" She wasn't actually surprised, but she just hadn't seen one. He hadn't been carrying a weapon when they'd undressed together. Surely she would have noticed the bulge under his jacket at some point over the past two days.

Two days… It felt like a lifetime since she'd had her little girl safe at home.

"I hope that's not a problem for you," he said. "We do not carry a weapon unless necessary. All agency field personnel are properly trained in the use of firearms for the purpose of protecting clients. Unfortunately, that step is sometimes essential in what we do."

"No." She held up both hands. "It's not a problem. I understand. I just hadn't noticed a weapon, so I assumed you didn't have one."

"My weapon is locked in a handgun safe in the trunk of my vehicle. I have an array of equipment, like video cameras and listening devices—much like the ones we found in your house—next door. Again, none of which I use unless necessary. From this point forward, being fully prepared for any possibility is, unfortunately, necessary."

"I'm glad you're fully prepared." She shook her head. "I certainly was not. I was living my life as if I had nothing to worry about except finishing the next story." What a mistake that had been.

In all the research she'd done into true crime cases, she should have been better prepared. Going forward, preparation was going to be her watchword. This nightmare had taught her a huge lesson about many things; paying better attention was at the top of that list.

"Let's make that call," he suggested, not allowing her to dwell on regret.

Brenda went to the living room and the table by the door and picked through her handbag until she found the agent's business card, then she walked back to the kitchen. She slid onto the stool and picked up her cell phone.

"Here goes." She entered the number and hit the call button. She held her breath through two rings. Was no one answering their phones today? It seemed as if everyone had her on Ignore.

The ringing stopped and a gruff voice barked, "Cummings."

"Agent Cummings, this is Brenda Devers." She held her breath so he wouldn't hear her rapid breathing while she waited for him to react. Her nerves were in a frenzy.

"Ms. Devers, if you're calling for an update, there's nothing new on this end. I have been briefed about your missing child and your talk with the intruder Detective Shelton picked up. So, it seems you are as well or more enlightened than I."

"No, I'm not calling about an update. I'm calling because I think I've found something important that Scott had hidden in my house. I really feel like you need to see it."

A moment's hesitation, then, "Have you called Detective Shelton?"

"No, I..." She sighed. "I don't know how to put this politely so I'm just going to say it. I don't trust Detective Shelton. He's been holding back so many details, and I just don't know about him. Besides, you work for the FBI. If you can't help me, no one can." She glanced at Ben, who was smiling. Evidently he was impressed with the way she had buttered up the fake special agent.

"What did you find, Ms. Devers?"

"I'm not sure what it is," she said, trying to sound uncertain and worried—both of which she was. "But it's several series of numbers and a list of names. Given the firm worked in investments, I'm thinking this is important."

Silence. She held Ben's gaze...her heart doing flip-flops.

"Can you read some of the numbers off to me or perhaps give me the names?"

"I really don't want to do this over the phone. Can you come to my house at seven? I'll give the paper to you and maybe this will be over for me."

More silence. He wasn't sure if he trusted her...but she'd given him no reason so far not to trust her.

Unable to do anything but hold her breath, she waited.

"I already have a meeting that will prevent me from meeting you at seven. How is eight for you?"

"Yes." She dragged in a breath. "Eight is fine. Thank you. I'll be waiting."

"What about your friend from the Colby Agency?"

"Ben?" She glanced at him. "No, I didn't show it to him. I haven't shown it to anyone yet. I wanted you to see it first."

"All right. Eight o'clock."

He ended the call before she could thank him. Brenda exhaled a big breath. "Done. He'll be here at eight."

"You did incredibly well. I'm certain he was utterly convinced."

His words and smile lifted her spirits. "I was thinking about all that happened this afternoon. The unanswered calls to Mallory, the visit to her mother's home and then the business at the police department—and the blonde after that. We never went to Mallory's house."

"You're right," Ben agreed. "We called her former boyfriend, but we didn't go to her home."

"We have some time." Brenda's anticipation started to build. "Should we see if she's there? I'm sure the police will go to her address at some point, but I don't see any reason we can't go right now. Maybe this whole thing is a mix-up." Yeah right. What it was, she fully understood, was another example of her trusting someone she shouldn't have—like Scott.

"Let's do it. Whether she's there or not," Ben suggested, "we can talk to neighbors. See what they have to say. Sometimes that's the best way to find out who visits a person and what sort of activities go on at their residence."

Brenda's hopes lifted. "That's a great idea."

"Come on." He nodded toward the door. "Let's grab my equipment bag next door and head out."

They locked up her place on the way out and walked through the cool night air to his. The small historic home next to hers was nearly identical to her own. Small, with creaky floors and imperfect plaster. It was all those little quirks that gave these century-plus-old homes character and charm, in Brenda's opinion.

Since Ben had only been staying in the house next to hers temporarily, there were no family photos on the walls or other personal items scattered about the decor. There was just the man and the things he had brought in a suitcase, a duffel and one garment bag. She walked through the house while he checked that he had everything they would need. It took all of five minutes, but it was long enough for her to run her fingers along the sleeve of a navy sports jacket hanging in the closet of the room where he slept. He wore long-sleeved Henley-type shirts with jeans and always a casual jacket. Comfortable leather loafers completed his wardrobe.

She wondered if he dressed the same when he was off duty.

Or maybe this was his off-duty attire. Also in the closet was a pair of running shoes. The man was fit for sure.

"Ready?" he asked from the doorway of his bedroom.

He didn't ask why she was there, he just smiled as if he were glad she was curious.

She was very curious, but measuring the man based on the contents of his bedroom just now was really about distracting herself from the reality that it had been more than twenty-four hours since she had spoken to her child. Worse, she had no idea where Janey was. It was the most terrifying feeling of uncertainty and loss.

"Yes." She pushed aside the emotion that wanted to paralyze her and left the room, followed him out of the house and to her garage, where his rental car was parked. He took a moment to check it closely for any sort of explosive or tracking device. He'd explained the need to her already, but she kept forgetting it had to be done. She couldn't keep a thought except for wanting to find her daughter.

It would take about ten or so minutes to drive to Mallory's town house. Brenda desperately hoped they would find answers there.

Wouldn't it be amazing if Janey and Mallory were at her place and her cell phone had died and all the questions Brenda had were nothing more than a misunderstanding?

She could dream.

Mallory Lawrence Residence
Four Mile Post Road
Huntsville, 6:50 p.m.

THERE WERE LIGHTS on in Mallory's town house. She had the end unit so there was no neighbor on the right side. Light shone through the front window as well as those on the end. Was it possible that she was home?

Brenda's heart rate accelerated as they followed the sidewalk to the front door. The plant in the concrete flowerpot next to the door was dead. The temperatures hadn't gotten so cold this season. More likely it had died from lack of water. Mallory would be the first to say she wasn't exactly a homebody, and she definitely lacked any semblance of a green thumb. Her mother had probably planted it since her daughter would never be bothered with sprucing up the place.

Mothers did those kinds of things in hopes of making life simpler or just more colorful for their children, even grown-up ones. Brenda couldn't imagine ever considering Janey anything but her little girl. She wanted to help her with her hair at her senior prom and her gown at her college graduation. Worry knotted in her belly. She wanted to watch her little girl grow up and become an amazing person.

Ben knocked on the door and it swung inward. But not because someone opened it… Apparently it had not been fully closed.

Brenda looked from the now open door to him. "Should we go in?" That cold, thick sensation of fear had started to travel through her again. This could not be good.

"I'll go first," he said.

She nodded. He was the one with the gun after all. And she was terrified at the idea of what they might find.

He stepped into the narrow entryway. "Mallory?"

Brenda did the same, coming up next to him and calling out, "Mallory?" The quiet made the creeping sensation of anxiety ooze onto her skin. "Janey?"

Ben reached back and closed the door. He glanced at her. "Stay behind me."

She nodded her understanding. Her throat was too tight to speak.

He walked beyond the short wall that separated the small entry from the living room. Brenda was right behind him as they moved deeper into the space. There was no one on the floor…no one lying across the sofa or in a chair. All was perfectly tidy. They moved on toward the kitchen. Brenda peered up to the second-floor landing as they passed the staircase. Dark up there. Like the living room, the kitchen was neat and organized. No dirty dishes in the sink. Nothing on the stove. Nobody about.

Ben walked to the refrigerator and looked inside. When he drew back, he said, "Milk, eggs, yogurt. The usual. Nothing expired." He withdrew a small pizza box. "The receipt—" he tapped the white ticket taped to the box "—is from yesterday. Cheese pizza."

"Janey was here then. Just yesterday." The possibility made her chest fill with hope. "She loves cheese pizza."

He smiled, gave her a nod. "She was."

With renewed purpose, they did a quick check of the laundry closet and small patio out back, then headed for the stairs. The carpet on the stairs and in the second-floor hall kept their steps quiet.

"Mallory?" Ben called out again.

"Janey?" Brenda held her breath, wished she would hear her daughter say, *Mommy?*

The first bedroom on the left, overlooking the street out front, was the largest and appeared to have an attached bathroom. From the door the room appeared clear. Tidy, like the rest of the house. They headed to the other side toward the adjoining bathroom, but the body lying on the floor on that side of the bed stopped them. Brenda drew up short, her breath catching in fear. But the short dark hair told her it wasn't Mallory. Thank God.

Moving closer, it was obviously a man. Gray peppered his dark hair. Ben crouched next to him and checked his pulse. His back was toward Brenda so she couldn't see his face. It wasn't Mallory's former boyfriend. He had blond hair. Could it be her father? Worry twisted inside Brenda.

"It's Cummings," Ben said as he looked up to meet her gaze. "He's been stabbed."

Brenda's hand went over her mouth. "What if he came here for Mallory and Janey?" If it was true that he worked for the cartel, he may have decided she was in the way... and that he wanted Janey for manipulating Brenda to do whatever he asked.

Her heart surged higher into her throat, and she rushed out of the room, uncertain of her ability to keep down whatever she'd eaten or drank last. Her gaze shifted to the door that led into the other room, and her knees nearly gave out. What if Mallory and her child were in there? Tied up... possibly injured or...worse.

What if Mallory was the friend Cummings had been staying with? He'd said he was staying with a friend that night he caught her and Ben in Scott's house. If that were the case, could it mean he and Mallory were working together? How was that possible? Brenda had known Mallory for two years. Surely that couldn't be. There had to be some misunderstanding... Maybe Mrs. Lawrence was growing senile and wrongfully thought the cabin had sold. Maybe...

Brenda had to see for herself what was in the only other room on this floor.

She forced one foot in front of the other until she reached the door, then she stalled. On the beige carpet next to the bed was a Barbie doll with purple hair. *Blossom.*

Her heart squeezed as she walked slowly across the room then bent down to pick up the doll. She traced the pad of her thumb over the outfit…the denim overalls and tie-dyed shirt Janey loved. The angel necklace was looped around and around the doll. If the cheese pizza wasn't proof enough, this confirmed it. Janey had been here.

"I'm calling Detective Shelton."

Brenda turned to where Ben waited at the door. She held up the doll. "Janey was here. This is her doll."

Ben was across the room in three long strides. He pulled her into his arms and held her tight. "This is a good thing," he murmured.

Brenda hadn't realized she was crying until he hugged her. Then she couldn't stop. She buried her face in his chest.

"She was here, Brenda," he said softly, "not somewhere far away. She was here just yesterday, maybe even earlier today." He drew back then and fixed his gaze on hers. "There is no indication of a struggle or injury anywhere in this house. There's only Cummings—if Mallory saw him as an enemy, she may have stabbed him to get away from him. To get Janey away from him."

Brenda swiped at the tears sliding down her cheeks. Hurt and anger roared through her, but somehow she nodded her understanding. "If it's okay, I want to search this room."

"I'll call Shelton, and then I'll help you search the whole place."

He made the call. Brenda was vaguely aware of his voice as she explored every inch of the small bedroom. Under the bed. Between the mattress and box spring. The closet. The drawers in the dresser. Beneath the heating and air-conditioning floor register and in the cavity that it covered. There was nothing else of Janey's in the room. Nothing else at all. No extra bed linens. No stored decor. Most people stored their rarely used items or out-of-season clothing in an extra closet. But there was nothing here.

Where in the world had Mallory taken Janey?

Chapter Nineteen

7:15 p.m.

When Ben had completed his call to Detective Shelton, he and Brenda performed a closer inspection of the main bedroom. He was careful to avoid the area immediately around the body. No need to bother with that side of the bed. There was no table or anything else there, just the man's body.

One of the pressing questions in Ben's mind was why Cummings was here. Was he staying here? Was Mallory the friend he mentioned knowing in the area? Not likely unless of course Mallory was employed by the cartel as well. But if he were staying here, where were the signs of this? Ben had found nothing that he could point to as belonging to the man. No toiletries in the bathroom. No clothes unless Brenda had found something in one of the drawers.

"The usual personal items, all Mallory's," Brenda said, as she closed the final drawer on the dresser. "I can't say if anything is missing."

"Nothing that may have belonged to Cummings?" he asked from the closet door.

"No. Nothing like that. Are you thinking he was staying here? I wondered that myself. He said he had a friend nearby when we spoke to him at Scott's house."

"It was a thought, yes." Ben completed his inspection of the closet. "There are empty hangers, suggesting some items might be missing. A couple of hangers are on the floor."

Brenda joined him at the small walk-in closet. "Mallory's a neat freak. She must have been in a hurry to leave them there."

"Along with the potential missing clothing, we have this." He pointed to the wood shelf above the rod. "There's dust on either side of an empty, dust-free space. My guess is that's where a large item, like an overnight bag or suitcase, was stored."

Brenda nodded. "Mallory obviously realized she had to get out of here." She glanced toward the bed. "But was it before or after she killed Cummings?"

"Very good question," Ben agreed. He followed her out of the small closet. "In the bathroom there was no toothbrush in the holder. No hairbrush lying on the counter. There's every reason to believe Mallory grabbed a few things and left." He shrugged. "Maybe in a hurry."

"I thoroughly searched the other bedroom," Brenda said. "Looks like that's all there is to learn up here." She glanced toward the bed again. "Unless the forensic people find something they probably won't tell us about."

"I checked the other bathroom on this floor. Nothing unexpected there either. Let's go downstairs and finish our search before Shelton arrives."

Downstairs there was nothing of Janey's in the living room. In the kitchen there was that pizza box in the fridge as well as her favorite fruit drink.

"Janey loves these goldfish crackers," Brenda announced, holding a small bag she had found in one of the cabinets over the sink.

In Ben's mind there was no question Janey had been here.

The only questions were, where had they gone and had the child been in the house when Cummings was murdered? The idea made Ben all the more furious at the man Brenda had married. Ben just didn't understand how a man could put his own child and her mother in such jeopardy.

Brenda closed the cabinet door and turned to him. "Why isn't the Jenner family dealing with any of this fallout? The accounts you and your colleague found are in my name. Maybe Tate Jenner did the same with his wife's name. And why did his wife decide to get an attorney—the same one the cartel guy, Lanier, is using?" She shook her head. "The Tate family cannot have been exempt from this."

Before Ben could go into his theory about the Jenners, there was a firm series of raps on the door. "We'll talk about this when we're out of here."

She drew in a deep breath. "Okay."

Shelton and the other detective, Truss, waited at the door. Behind them was a line of other official personnel. Ben had no idea how the man rallied a team together in such a short time. Most cops had to wait for the various elements of the investigative team to arrive on scene. Not Shelton; he came locked and loaded.

He and Brenda were deposed to the living room while Shelton and Truss rushed upstairs to have a look at the body and the primary scene. Ben could see Brenda's anxiety growing. She wanted to discuss her concerns related to the Jenners. She was anxious to move forward. To do something. Her child was missing, and she was beside herself. But the uniformed officer who'd been left in the room with them prevented any such discussions. No need to give Shelton a heads-up on their thoughts or their plans.

When Shelton descended the stairs and came into the living room, the other officer took his leave. The detective sat down in a chair closer to Brenda than to Ben. She was the one he hoped to learn the most from. He took out his notepad and started his questioning.

"How did the two of you end up here?"

Brenda looked to Ben, and he said, "Since Brenda has been unable to reach Mallory, I felt it was imperative that we visit her home to see if she was here."

Shelton grunted a sound of acknowledgment or something of that order. "Why didn't you do that before?" Again, he directed this query at Brenda.

"In case you've forgotten," Ben intercepted, drawing the detective's attention back to him, "we've been a little busy. We were actually headed here when Brenda was called to speak with Lanier."

His gaze narrowing with mounting suspicion, Shelton asked, "Have either of you had contact with Special Agent Cummings since he found you trespassing at the home of Scott Devers?"

"No," Ben said honestly. "Not until this evening. Since you had no updates from him during our last meeting, Brenda was eager to know if the agent had discovered anything new that might help with the search for her daughter."

"Have you heard anything?" Brenda demanded, her hands clasped on the handbag in her lap. "Surely there's been some response to the Amber Alert."

"We've had no credible responses so far, ma'am," he assured her, which Ben doubted was any assurance at all. He turned to Ben then. "You were saying Ms. Devers called Agent Cummings. In my office you suggested I should call Cummings's superior. Well, I did that, and guess what?"

Ben assumed this was a rhetorical question.

"There is no Agent Jarrod Cummings." Shelton harrumphed. "But you knew that, didn't you, Mr. Clark?"

"I had my suspicions."

Shelton glanced at Brenda then. "You called Agent Cummings."

"She did," Ben responded. "Her child is missing, and we'll take any help we can get to find her."

Since phone records were all too easy to obtain, Ben saw no reason not to divulge the information. Giving Shelton a reason to suspect them of something related to Cummings's murder would prove problematic. When it came to moments like this, omissions were the same as lies.

"And he asked you to meet him here," Shelton said, looking from one to the other.

"No." There the detective went hoping to trip them up. "During the call," Ben explained patiently, "Cummings agreed to a meeting at Brenda's home at eight. Since we had some time before his arrival, we decided to come by and see if perhaps Mallory might be here hiding for some reason."

"We," Shelton said pointedly, "were scheduled to come here. We were only waiting for the warrant. You see, Mr. Clark, unlike private investigators, we have rules and procedure to follow. We can't just bust in and claim the door was open."

"We couldn't wait," Brenda spoke up. "My child is missing. Rules and procedure were not on my mind."

Shelton cleared his throat, glanced at his notepad. "Did either of you do any searching of the house, in particular the room where the body was found?"

Ben gave a confirming nod. "We walked through every room looking for any sign Janey had been here." Their prints would be found, no need to deny this.

"Did you find anything?" Shelton asked. He looked from Ben to Brenda.

Her fingers tightened on her handbag where she had

tucked Janey's purple-haired Barbie. "Her favorite pizza and juice are in the refrigerator, and the goldfish crackers she likes are in the cabinet. That suggests to me that she was here."

"Had you ever allowed your daughter to come to Mallory's house in the past?" Shelton shot back.

"No." Brenda shrugged. "I can't say that Scott didn't allow her to come over to Mallory's when I was traveling, but I haven't gone anywhere overnight in the past year—except the trip to Los Angeles that you already know about."

"So she could have been here during that time," Shelton suggested.

"That's possible," Brenda agreed, "but Mallory never mentioned it, and usually Janey tells all about her adventures with Mallory. And the receipt on the pizza box is from yesterday."

Ben hoped the little girl was seeing this time away from her mother as just another adventure with her nanny. If one or both had been harmed… He wasn't going there. Not yet. There was still every reason to believe the child was safe. He suspected that would be the case as long as the cartel or persons responsible for her abduction needed her for leverage.

Shelton closed his notepad. "If I have more questions, I'll call. The coroner will be here soon, so it's better if the two of you go home. I think you've done enough *investigating* for one evening."

Brenda stood. Ben followed suit. When they would have started for the door, she hesitated. "I have a question for you."

Shelton heaved himself to his feet. "If I have an answer I will share it with you." There was no enthusiasm in the words.

"What about Lena Jenner? Are you investigating her the way you are me?"

Good question. Ben should have asked, but it was better coming from Brenda.

Shelton looked surprised at the subject of the question. "Do you have some reason to believe I should be investigating her?"

"Tate and Scott were partners," Brenda tossed back at him. "Doesn't that make the possibility that she knows something as likely as the possibility that I do?"

Shelton nodded slowly as if needing time to make his response more palatable. "It does. What you don't know is that Agent Cummings focused on Jenner's wife while I focused on you. We felt it was the best way to cover all bases. But I assure you, she didn't get off any easier. At least I assume she didn't. With what we've learned about Cummings, I can't be certain of his activities. Which just means I will have to follow up. So, to answer your question, if she hasn't already felt the weight of this investigation, she will soon."

"Thank you for telling me."

Once they were outside, Ben scanned the street for a vehicle that may have belonged to Cummings. There were several. He supposed Shelton's people would have to figure out that part. At his rental, he turned on the flashlight app of his phone and checked the car doors, peered at length under the body of the car then had a look under the hood. Once he was satisfied all was clear, he unlocked the passenger compartment and checked the interior.

"You can get in now," he said to Brenda, who stood by patiently as she did every time he performed this safety check. Once she was inside, he walked around to the driver's side and got in.

Not until they were driving away did a rush of words

burst out of her. "I really want to go see Lena Jenner now. I can't get the idea out of my head that her using the same attorney—Harris Carlisle—as Dirk Lanier means something relevant to all this. I want to talk to her before she disappears too."

Ben glanced at her. There hadn't been time to go into this before when Brenda brought up the prospect of looking more closely at the partner's wife. "I have Max checking up on Lena Jenner. Like you," he confirmed, "I'm not a fan of coincidences. We did a preliminary in the beginning but found nothing. It's time for a deeper dig."

Brenda turned in her seat. "What if Lena has been looking for Mallory and Janey and was here when Cummings showed up? She may have killed him. I really want to go to her house. Now. Right now. We might even catch her in the act of washing blood off her hands."

Ben glanced at her. "No wonder your books are so well-done. You think like a detective." He laughed. "Or maybe a criminal."

Brenda smiled and he was glad he'd had something to do with it.

"We're going to find your daughter."

She nodded and resettled in her seat.

Ben was determined that whoever had started this thing, he intended to end it.

Chapter Twenty

Jenner Residence
Carnoustie Lane
Huntsville, 9:30 p.m.

Brenda was out of the car before Ben could round the hood. She stared up at the multistory home, her frustration building. Like Scott, Tate Jenner had chosen a home on the prestigious Ledges. Closer to the golf course, naturally.

The garage doors were shut so they had no way to determine if Lena's SUV was here. But there were lights on in the house. Brenda had only been to the Jenner home on a few occasions. Christmas parties, mostly. Only once here, maybe two years ago. An anniversary party for the couple, which, she assumed, was mostly because they had wanted to show off their new home.

The house was a carefully balanced blend of rustic country and elegance. The wraparound porches provided the country touch to the exterior. Inside were acres of wide plank wood flooring showcased by smooth white walls and rustic, natural beadboard. It was all very stately and large. But that didn't mean there weren't secrets hiding in the dark corners. All this time she had trusted the man she married to be the husband she thought he was. She'd trusted these people to be who they presented themselves to be.

When had money become more important than the lives of others?

Anger beat in her veins, keeping time with the thud of her heart. She was sick to death of the lies…at the end of her rope with worry about Janey. She needed answers, and by God she intended to have them.

Ben pressed the doorbell. This one had an intricately carved brass piece surrounding the lit button, but not the sort that provided a live feed of who was at the door or the ability to communicate with them. She supposed such a high-tech device didn't fit with the character of the home.

The door opened and seven-year-old Trek stood there.

"Don't open the door!" The seemingly disembodied words floated from somewhere deeper in the house. Brenda recognized the voice as Lena's.

"Hi, Trek." Brenda barged past him.

The boy stared up at her. "Mom's in the kitchen." His dark eyes were wide and uncertain as if it was past his bedtime, but something kept him awake. He also probably understood, too late, that his mother would be angry that he'd opened the door.

"This is my friend Ben," Brenda said as she continued forward, Ben beside her now.

The door closed and Trek rushed past them and shot up the stairs. Smart kid. He didn't want to be down here when the proverbial poop hit the fan.

The entry hall cut through the center of the house from the front door to the kitchen. The rooms on either side were enormous. A grand living room, dining room and picturesque library. But it was the kitchen that focused on entertaining. It ran the full width of the house…opened onto an equally large terrace with a pool and all manner of small, luxurious seating and entertaining niches tucked into the landscape beyond it.

On the right side of the kitchen, far from all else, were two doors. One led to a pantry—the word was etched into the glass—and the other to the triple-car garage. The door to the garage stood open, and Lena had just walked through and reached for a suitcase. Two more of a matching luggage set stood next to the door. Her long blond hair tucked up in a claw clasp, she wore jeans and a T-shirt. So un-Lena-like. Brenda couldn't help scrutinizing the pink tee for blood splatter or smears.

Lena was preparing to disappear.

She and Ben were just in time. Brenda had expected as much. "Hi, Lena. Going somewhere?"

The other woman allowed a moment of shock to flash across her face, but it quickly shifted to indignation. "What are you doing here?"

The emotions that charged through Brenda then almost undid her, but she snatched back control. "I guess you haven't heard. My daughter is missing?"

Lena blinked but not quickly enough to hide her obvious surprise. "I had no idea..."

Barely able to hold back the rush of outrage, Brenda decided to give her something to think about. "I'm certainly glad your child is safe and sound at home with you. When this happens, it's the not knowing that's the most terrifying."

Lena's chin went up. "Whatever happened to your child is not my fault. I was smart enough not to get involved in the mess our husbands left behind."

Brenda laughed long and loud. When she finally regained her composure, she said simply, "I didn't have a choice."

"Well, you have no one but Scott to blame for that." She

reached for one of the suitcases on the floor. "Now, if you'll excuse me, my son and I are preparing for our annual trip to Miami."

"Funny," Brenda countered, "I've never heard of those annual trips. I thought you preferred Barbados. Did your attorney approve your travel? Oh." Brenda made a knowing face. "Were you aware he's also representing the cartel thug who broke into my house? Sounds like you might be more involved than you realize."

"I have no idea what you're talking about." She glanced at Ben. "Who is this?"

"Ben Clark," he answered. "I'm with the Colby Agency of Chicago. I'm investigating this case."

She looked taken aback by the news. Had she not heard? Cummings wasn't keeping her informed?

"How dare you bring a stranger into my home," she snapped. "How do you know this man is who he says he is? It's exactly this sort of naivete that has you in trouble, Brenda."

"Because I confirmed who he is." Brenda took a step in her direction. "He is the only person in all of this who's helping me find the truth—everyone else is either lying to me or hiding the truth."

"Why would I believe *you*?"

"I don't care what you believe." Brenda was done with trying to explain. "But did you know that someone from the cartel shot your husband *before* the explosion? That one of the people at the office when that explosion happened was an FBI agent? At least we think he was. Considering what we know about Agent Cummings, we can't be sure."

Lena froze, that paralyzed-by-terror expression on her face. "What do you mean?"

Brenda turned to Ben. "Should we tell her?"

Ben shrugged. "I suspect she already knows. She just wants to see if you actually know."

"Oh." Brenda turned back to the woman whose child had played with her own on so many occasions. "Cummings works for the cartel. The same one that shot your husband and blew up the firm. The one who is threatening me and who took my daughter hostage."

"You can't prove any of this," Lena argued.

"I can't," Brenda admitted. "But I'm sure Detective Shelton will figure it out while he's investigating the man's murder."

This time Lena grabbed at the door facing as if the news had shaken her balance. "What're you talking about?"

"The man who called himself Agent Jarrod Cummings is dead, Ms. Jenner," Ben warned. "If the people who sent him couldn't protect him or turned on him for some reason, how do you know the same thing won't happen to you?"

"If you know anything," Brenda urged, "about who took my daughter, you need to tell me. Please."

"I don't know anything about your daughter." Lena turned to go back into the garage.

Ben walked to the door, picked up the last of the suitcases and joined her. "You won't be able to get away from them, Ms. Jenner. These aren't the sort of people you can outrun."

Brenda waited at the door, listening to the exchange in hopes Lena would break down and say something helpful.

Lena stared at Brenda as Ben put the suitcases in the back of her SUV. "You don't understand," she argued. "You have no idea what I had to promise them…what I had to do to protect my son."

Her eyes widened as if she'd only just considered that she hadn't seen or heard him in several minutes.

"He went upstairs," Brenda explained.

Lena glared at her. "You need to leave." She turned to Ben. "Now."

Ben walked toward Brenda. "She's right. We should go. She can't help us."

Brenda wanted to argue, but defeat had punched her hard in the gut. She took one last long look at Lena before walking away.

Before they reached the front door, Trek rushed down the stairs and headed to the kitchen. Brenda fought back the tears. She refused to cry right now. She had to be strong. She had to find Janey.

Ben said nothing as they walked back to his car. She waited while he performed the necessary check before getting into the passenger seat. A whole minute of painful silence elapsed as they drove down the twisty mountain road.

When she couldn't take it anymore, Brenda asked, "Why didn't we stay and follow her or something?"

She didn't want to be disappointed in the decision Ben had made, but she was. She was certain Lena knew more than she had shared.

He slowed near the guard shack to wait for the gate to open, and then at the traffic signal he stopped. He picked up his cell and opened an app. A map appeared with a red dot blinking in the center of the screen. "That," he explained, "is the tracking device I placed in her vehicle. We'll wait in the parking lot across the street and follow her."

Brenda wanted to hug him. The relief gushing through her almost made speech impossible. "Thank you. Thank you so much."

"We've got this, Brenda."

For the first time since this nightmare started, she thought they just might.

Target Parking Lot
Carl T Jones Drive
Huntsville, 10:20 p.m.

BEN SHUT OFF the engine. The headlights went dark, leaving only the streetlamps scattered across the parking lot to chase away the darkness. Brenda needed Lena Jenner to lead her to wherever Janey was being held. Maybe she was a fool to believe that was a possibility, but she was desperate. They were out of options.

There was no one left to turn to.

If Scott was still alive—despite what Lanier had said—and wasn't actively helping with the search for Janey…

Brenda exiled the thought. Even Scott wouldn't do that to his own daughter.

On the other hand, he had pretended to be dead and allowed his child to grieve him. What kind of father did that? She had to stop giving him any sort of credit. The man had obviously put money above all else and now this was the result.

Even if she found Janey, the two of them might never be safe again.

Her cell vibrated against her thigh. If it was Detective Shelton…

Mallory.

The bottom dropped out of Brenda's stomach. "It's Mallory." She accepted the call. "Mallory, where are you? Where is Janey? I need to speak to her!"

Ben leaned closer to hear the other side of the conversation. Brenda should have set the call to speaker, but she'd been too startled to think and now she was afraid to do anything that might cause the call to drop.

"You've made this far more complicated than it needed to

be, Brenda, with all your running to the cops and prompting an Amber Alert."

The anger in the other woman's voice startled Brenda all over again. Her first instinct was to demand how she thought she had the right to say such a thing. But that would be a mistake. She had to be careful, keep her talking. Stay on her good side—assuming she had one. Brenda had once believed her to be a good person…a good friend.

"I'm sorry, Mallory," she offered in hopes of assuaging her anger. "I didn't know what else to do. Please," she pleaded, "just tell me if my baby is okay."

"Janey is fine."

Brenda's eyes closed in gratitude. *Thank God. Thank God.*

"But you have something I need. I know you have it because someone attempted to access the accounts."

Brenda looked to Ben. It must have been his colleague Max. "I don't understand. What do you mean?"

"If you want to see your child again, you'd better not play that game with me. I want those account numbers and the names. I know you have them."

The only way Mallory could know about what Brenda had found was if Cummings had told her. Just because someone had attempted to access the accounts didn't mean it was Brenda. It could have been Scott or Lena. Did that mean Mallory had killed the fake special agent? Brenda's heart twisted with fear. She didn't want to believe the woman she had trusted with the care of her child was a murderer. But denying the possibility was growing harder and harder.

She looked to Ben in question. What should she do?

He nodded for her to go ahead.

"I found the list today," she admitted. "Scott must have hidden it in my house. I had no idea, but all those messages telling me I'd better hurry up and find what they wanted had me tearing the house apart."

"I sent you those messages," she snarled. "Took you long enough to get the job done."

"I'm sorry," Brenda implored. "I did the best I could."

"I searched your house a dozen times," Mallory countered, her voice dripping with suspicion now, "and I never found it. You'd better not be lying to me."

"The first name on the list is Albert Winthrop," Brenda told her. "Does that sound familiar?"

The silence that followed had new fear trickling through her.

"Oh yeah." Mallory laughed. "That's the one Scott screwed up—the stupid mistake that got him caught. Winthrop is the reason we're in this mess. It's him you have to thank for all this."

Brenda wondered if she meant Mr. Winthrop or Scott. Maybe both. "He's dead."

More silence.

Then, "Who's dead?"

"Mr. Winthrop. He was in a car accident."

"This is what we're going to do," Mallory went on without acknowledging the statement. "I will call you with a location. You will bring the list to me. I don't want anything sent via email or text. I don't even want you to say anything else over the phone. I need you to hand deliver it."

"Wait," Brenda argued, her bravado finding its legs once more. "I'm not giving you anything until you give me Janey."

"You are in no position to make demands," Mallory fired back. "Now pay attention or you'll never see her again."

"You better not hurt my child," Brenda warned, a fresh burst of outrage getting the better of her.

"Why would I hurt a cute kid like Janey? She's far too valuable on the black market to damage in any way."

A new kind of horror poured like ice-cold acid through Brenda, freezing and scalding at the same time. "Just tell me what to do."

"That's more like it," Mallory said smugly. "I'll call with a location, and you'll come. *Alone*. You give me the list and I'll give you the kid. We go our separate ways. End of story."

"Okay," Brenda agreed without hesitation. "How long before you'll call?" Her pulse was pounding like a drum in her ears. Her heart thumped wildly.

"A couple of hours maybe. I have some details to work out. Meanwhile, you stay cool and do not talk to anyone. Do you understand me? No one!"

"Yes," Brenda urged. "Please, just let me hear her voice. I only want to tell her I love her. Please."

A big, exasperated exhale. "Don't say or ask anything your child will regret," Mallory warned.

Brenda held her breath, her gaze locked on Ben's. He squeezed her hand. She hadn't even realized he'd been holding her hand. She was so grateful he was here.

"Hello."

The sound of Janey's sweet voice had tears of joy spilling from Brenda's eyes. "Hey, sweetie. How are you? Mommy misses you so much."

"Me and Mall'y are having an adventure," she announced.

"Wow, I hope you're having fun."

"We're having lots of fun." She made a soft sound like a sleepy sigh. "I miss you too, Mommy. When are you coming to pick me up?"

"Very soon," Brenda promised. The struggle to keep her voice steady was an immense one. "I love you, baby girl."

"Wuv you too."

"Satisfied?" Mallory had reclaimed the phone.

"Yes." Brenda swiped at her eyes. "Thank you for taking good care of her." Janey sounded contented…and safe. Unaware of any danger.

"You'll hear from me when I'm ready to meet."

The call ended.

Brenda dropped her phone into her lap and sobbed into her hands. Her child was alive… She was okay…

For now.

Chapter Twenty-One

10:50 p.m.

Ben reached across the console and pulled Brenda into his arms. There were things he wanted to say but none of those words would change what she was feeling. She was desperate, nearly beaten and yet hopeful because the woman holding Janey hostage had allowed Brenda to hear her voice.

She drew back, swiped at her eyes. He wished he had a handkerchief or tissues, but he had nothing like that in this rental car.

"Sorry about that. I'm okay." She took a deep breath and resettled in her seat. "This is a definite step forward, right?"

"Yes. Mallory has made contact and laid out her demands. You have agreed to meet them. Now we wait for her next call."

Brenda sniffed. "She said I had to come alone."

"That's the usual protocol kidnappers put on the table. But don't worry. We'll figure that part out as soon as we know the location."

Ben's cell shimmied in the cup holder. He reached for it and checked the screen. *Max.* He opened the text box.

Found active payments from Lawrence to a house on Mariposa Road.

Ben asked for the house number and thanked him for the good work. Once he had the number he entered the location into his maps app and reviewed the directions. Not so far from here.

"We have another address with an active account connected to Mallory. It's very near the Bradley house where we found the second message."

"Are we going there?" Brenda asked, her voice hopeful.

He nodded. "We are." His phone shimmied again. This time it was the tracking app. "Lena Jenner is on the move."

Brenda groaned. "What do we do? Follow Lena or go to this house?"

Ben considered their options. "We don't know with any measure of certainty that Lena is involved with Mallory. She didn't appear to be aware that Janey was even missing."

"You're right." Brenda nodded. "Let's go to the Mariposa address. Mallory and Janey could be there right now."

A left turn out of the parking lot and they followed Airport Road until it transitioned into Johnson Road. A right on Triana Boulevard took them back to the Merrimack Mill Village area. A few more turns and they arrived on Mariposa.

"That's it." Brenda pointed to the house coming up on the right.

Ben slowed and pulled to the curb two houses before the one that was their target. There were no vehicles in the driveway or nearby on the street. No lights in the house.

"What if this was just a distraction?" Brenda chewed her lip. "That text did come just before Lena left her house."

"I know it looks that way," Ben said patiently, "but trust me, Max knows what he's doing. If he says there's activity on the property related to Mallory, he's done a check of the payment history. It won't have been just a sudden transaction, or he would have warned me."

"Sorry." Brenda shook her head. "I'm just…overwhelmed."

"No explanation necessary." Ben hitched his head toward the house. "Let's check it out. Even if Mallory and Janey aren't here, there may be evidence that will help us trace their movements."

They emerged from the car and moved along the sidewalk until they reached the house. It was a one-story with large windows. Ben walked straight to the door and knocked. Brenda peeked through a window.

"It's dark in there, but I think it might be empty," she reported in a stage whisper. "Maybe a sofa or a love seat in the middle of the room."

Ben checked the door. Locked. "Let's walk around back." He wasn't opposed to breaking and entering when necessary, but it was best not to do it where you were likely to be seen by neighbors.

They moved around to the back of the house. The yard was fairly small. A bit overgrown with a rickety privacy fence—all worked in their favor. Brenda moved in close to the windows, attempting to see beyond one after the other. Ben walked straight to the rear entrance. A sliding glass patio door. He gave it a tug and, to his surprise, it slid open.

"Here we go."

When Brenda joined him, he reminded her, "Stay behind me until we've ensured the house is clear of potential threat."

"Got it."

He walked in, she followed. He slid the door closed once more. The rear entrance brought them into a small kitchen. He tried a light switch, then another. Apparently the utilities had been shut off. He used the flashlight app on his cell phone to scan the room. Clear. The interior was in need of a new coat of paint on the walls but otherwise unremarkable.

Beyond the kitchen was an L-shaped living-dining room combo. There was a sofa but no other furniture or indication of occupancy. The place was surprisingly clean. Off the living room was a narrow hall. The first door on the left was a bathroom. Empty. Nothing in the cabinet over the sink or in the one beneath.

The first bedroom on the right was very small. No furniture. No indication anyone had been there recently. Brenda checked the closet.

"Empty." She hugged herself, chafed her arms. "Looks like the whole place is empty except for that sofa in the living room."

"Let's see the rest."

The next door on the right was another bedroom. It too was the same as the first one. One remaining door on the left. Unlike with the other rooms, this door was shut. The closed door put Ben on alert. He glanced at Brenda, and she stepped behind him.

He opened the door and had a look. The beam of light bumped over something on the floor. Ben moved in closer. A blanket was spread over a lump there. The shape of the lump suggested it was likely a body.

Brenda gasped, and before he could stop her, she had propelled herself around him and pulled back the blanket.

Male.

Scott Devers.

Evidently Dirk Lanier had been right.

Brenda stood over her dead husband's body, her hands pressed to her mouth.

Ben moved to her side and ushered her into the hall. He

leaned her against the wall. "Stay here. I'll have a closer look and call Shelton."

Ben entered the bedroom once more and used the flashlight app to get a better look. He felt for a pulse although it was clear the man was dead. His body wasn't as cold as he'd expected so he examined his fingers and hands. No indication of rigor mortis just yet. He couldn't have been dead very long. Maybe an hour, two tops.

Next he surveyed the body for injury. There was blood on the front of his shirt. But he had not been stabbed like Cummings. He'd been shot, twice. Once in the abdomen, and the second shot, likely the kill shot, had entered the chest very close to the heart.

Moving quickly, he checked the pockets of his jeans as best he could without moving the body. He hoped to find a cell phone, but it was not there. He scanned the room. No weapon. No phone.

Ben looked in the closet then, but the room was clear save for the body in the middle of the floor.

He walked back into the hall where Brenda waited. "He hasn't been dead long. An hour or two maybe."

Brenda squeezed her eyes shut. "He and Cummings…" She shook her head. "They were both found in properties belonging to Mallory. If she would think nothing of killing two people…"

"You and Mallory have a deal. She isn't going to risk hurting Janey until she has what she needs."

"Hope not." Brenda hugged herself more tightly.

Ben wanted to hold her and comfort her, but there wasn't time just now. They couldn't be sure when Mallory would make contact again. "I have to call Shelton. We should probably wait outside until he arrives."

Brenda followed him to the front door. Ben unlocked it

and they walked out. He made the call and tucked the phone back into his pocket.

Now they waited.

Brenda leaned against the front door. He glanced at her, wished he knew the right thing to say to alleviate her worry.

"I know this is hard," he confessed. "Is there anything I can do?"

She shook her head. "The only thing we can do is wait for word from Mallory."

They waited a minute or two more in silence. Then the distant sound of sirens and traffic filled the darkness.

"You know," she said, "I keep thinking I'll wake up and find that this has all been a dream. But when I open my eyes each morning it just keeps going."

Ben put his arm around her and pulled her close. He kissed the top of her head.

Headlights bobbed in the distance. Another set and then another followed that.

"Looks like Shelton and his crew have arrived." He dropped his arm to his side, not wanting to give Shelton something else to pick at.

The detective squealed to a stop at the curb and was out of his car before it stopped rocking.

"This is getting to be a pattern," he announced as he approached, his shuffle weary.

Ben had warned him when he called that there was no electricity so they would need auxiliary lighting. "Maybe we're just really good at finding the missing pieces of this case."

Shelton snorted a laugh. Then he frowned and fished his phone from his pocket. "Shelton," he barked in answer.

Ben glanced at Brenda, gave her a reassuring smile.

Shelton swore repeatedly, thanked the caller and then shoved his phone back into his pocket.

"Well, Ms. Devers, looks like you might be the last one standing."

She straightened away from the door. "What do you mean?"

"That was an officer at the scene of a car accident on the other side of Chapman Mountain. He called me because I have an alert on the players related to this case. The driver involved is Lena Jenner. She's alive but in bad shape."

"What about her son?" Brenda asked, her voice strained with worry.

"He's banged up but stable."

"Do you know what happened?" Ben decided not to mention anything about the tracking device. Not just now anyway.

Shelton shook his head. "No other cars involved. She was probably driving too fast. Crashes like that happen on that stretch of road going over the mountain all the time."

Shelton was right then… Brenda was the last one standing.

Ben would not allow anyone to get to her.

Chapter Twenty-Two

Friday, May 8
Mariposa Road
Huntsville, 1:30 a.m.

Brenda was sick with worry. It was half past one and Mallory had not called back. Did she have some way of knowing they were here at this house—the house where Scott had been murdered—surrounded by police?

She stood in the corner of the living room. This was where Shelton had sequestered them it felt like forever ago. Brenda closed her eyes. She wanted her child. She wanted her life back.

"Excuse me, Ms. Devers."

Her breath caught as she pulled back from the troubling thoughts. The new special agent from the FBI, this one supposedly real, had appeared in front of her. What was his name? Lance something. English. Yes, that was it. The man was painfully young. Was he even old enough to be an FBI agent?

"Yes?" She glanced around in search of Ben. He'd gone to find Shelton and ask why they hadn't been allowed to leave.

"I wanted to give you an update about your daughter."

Thank God. One of the things she'd asked Shelton while

he took their statements was why she hadn't heard anything else from the Amber Alert. Wasn't a parent supposed to be kept informed? As for getting excited about whatever he had to say, there was no point. She knew who had her daughter and she couldn't say a word to this man or to Shelton.

"There have been numerous calls and even a few sightings, but none have panned out," the agent explained. "But the Bureau is working with Huntsville PD in an effort to find your daughter. You and I, however, need to discuss preparing for the potential of a ransom demand. No one has called you as of yet, is that correct?"

For one instant—a single uncertain moment—she wanted to tell him. But she reminded herself that the other FBI agent, the murdered one, had faked his way into this case. And in truth she still wasn't certain that she could trust Detective Shelton, or anyone else for that matter.

"That's correct."

"Could we arrange a time to meet at your home and see what we can do? We'll put a wiretap on your phone."

"Sure. I would appreciate that." She might as well make her response sound authentic.

"How about two this afternoon? I can have a small team together by then to get the ball rolling."

"That sounds good. Thank you." If she were lucky, by then she would have Janey back and Mallory would be just a bad memory.

"All right. I'll see you then." He walked back into the kitchen, where Shelton seemed to be holding a discussion with his people.

Hopefully Ben would get an answer soon as to whether they could leave. They'd given their statements. There was no reason for them to still be here. Brenda closed her eyes again and thought of her baby's sweet voice on the phone a few hours ago. She hoped Mallory called back soon. Then again what good would it do if—

"Detective Shelton says we can go now."

The sound of Ben's voice jerked her to attention. "Thank God."

She followed Ben to the door. "Did he mention if he'd heard anything else about Lena and Trek?"

"Trek is fine, but Lena is in a coma. Her condition has improved somewhat but is still guarded. It's not unusual for a patient with such severe trauma to remain in a coma for a time, allowing the body to focus on healing."

Brenda went out the door first. When he'd joined her, she said, "Shelton didn't tell you that, did he?"

Ben smiled, this one-sided expression that made her feel safe and warm despite current circumstances. "I had a colleague check into the situation."

The Colby Agency seemed to have all sorts of connections or people capable of finding the necessary contacts in record time. She was immensely grateful for their support.

The one good thing Scott did, she thought again.

"Thank you." As much as Brenda resented Lena for whatever part she had played in all this, she didn't wish anything like this on her. Her son needed her.

Ben conducted his usual check of his rental car before they climbed in. Once they were on their way, he said, "You should be hearing from Mallory soon. We'll go back to your house. I'll walk you in, see that all is as it should be, then I'll go next door."

"You think maybe she's watching the house. Waiting until I'm there, maybe alone, to make her move?"

"It's possible. The police are distracted elsewhere. I didn't notice a tail at any point yesterday other than York. I think you may have fallen lower in Shelton's priorities given all that's happened. That gives us an opportunity to present you as being alone."

Brenda felt sick to her stomach at the idea that had just formed in her head. "You don't think Mallory killed Scott just to draw the police away?"

Scott was really dead…like Lanier told her. No, not right. He hadn't been dead that long. Some tiny sliver of her brain wanted to be sad and to grieve, but Brenda couldn't. And it wasn't even because she had cried way too much over the man already. It was because every part of her was focused on her daughter… Finding Janey was everything. It was all that mattered.

"No." Ben glanced at her. "She couldn't be sure we would discover this other house. I think Lena Jenner's car crash may have been the distraction."

If that proved true, then obviously Mallory had no care for who she killed—even a child. Fear fired in Brenda's blood. There went the idea that Janey might actually be safe with her. But then she recalled the comment about the black market. Cutting the woman any sort of slack was a waste of time.

"What you're saying is that with Shelton and the new FBI agent distracted, she feels comfortable maybe coming to my home. But she knows about you."

Worry gnawed at Brenda. If Mallory had a plan like that…how would they ever manage to outwit her? She surely wouldn't come alone. Then again, Scott was dead. Cummings was dead. The cartel guy who had shown up at the office the day of the explosion was dead—it was apparently his body they had mistaken for Scott's. The intruder, Dirk Lanier, was in jail. Unless he'd made bond with the help of his high-profile attorney.

It didn't matter, she realized. There could be dozens of them here or coming.

Defeat sucked at her. She looked to the man driving. But she had a secret weapon. She had the Colby Agency.

"She knows about me, yes," Ben said in answer to her comment. "We're setting a trap for her—one she won't see coming. If she shows, we'll be ready for her."

"So I'll go in my house and you'll go in yours," Brenda suggested, wanting details. "Let her believe the circumstances are the same as before she left." She supposed that would work. Mallory probably had no idea she and Ben had spent a night together.

"Yes." He glanced at her. "But don't worry, I'll be close."

"Okay. I'm ready to do this."

All they needed was for Mallory to actually show up.

Devers Residence
White Street
Huntsville, 2:30 a.m.

BRENDA WALKED INTO her house and waited while Ben had a look around. The survey took longer than she'd expected, but she was tired. She wasn't so sure she could trust her judgment of time. Her body needed sleep, but her mind would not allow it.

Not until she had Janey home.

Once he was satisfied the house was clear, he gave her arm a squeeze. "Good night. Try to get some sleep."

"I'll try," she promised. His suggestion was for anyone who might be listening. While they were gone more listening devices could have been planted in her home.

He left, and she closed the door, locked it and just stood there wondering what to do next.

It had been four hours since Mallory called.

What if she never called back? What if…

Brenda couldn't do that to herself. Deep breath. She needed a way to keep herself occupied until whatever was going to happen, happened. A cup of tea would be good. She had a variety of teas. She used to drink it every afternoon, but in recent months she'd basically given up all those small, simple pleasures. She had to get back to that. When Janey was back home, things were going back to the way they should be. No more dwelling on Scott…

Dear God, she had to bury him again. Explaining that to Janey should be fun.

As she lit the flame under the kettle, she considered that at some point in the next day or two she needed to let her agent know that her next project might be a few weeks late. She'd always been on time—surely she was due one failure to meet her deadline.

On top of that there were upcoming meetings about the movie. She so wanted to be celebrating…but how could she?

A soft knock at the back door drew her attention there.

Had Ben forgotten something? She walked to the door. Didn't dare turn on an exterior light. She peered through the glass, hoping the stars and moonlight would be enough…

Janey stood on the porch staring up at her.

For a moment Brenda was certain she had imagined her, then she waved and said, "Mommy, open the door."

Heart thundering, Brenda yanked at the door. It was locked. Her fingers fumbled with the lock. She wrenched the door open, reached down, and her daughter ran into her arms.

"Oh my God. Oh my God," she murmured, her eyes closing in relief. She inhaled the familiar scent of her child's hair and held her soft body close against her.

"Take it inside."

Brenda's eyes flew open. Mallory stood maybe two feet away, a gun in her hand.

A new surge of fear had Brenda moving quickly, Janey in her arms. She stepped back into the house. Mallory came in, closed the door behind her.

"You have your daughter," she said. "Now where's that list?"

BEN HAD BEEN waiting for the moment when he heard Mallory's voice.

Once he had checked Brenda's home when they arrived and left the listening devices necessary for keeping him apprised of whatever was happening inside, he'd come home. Made a show of turning on lights and the television. He'd grabbed a washcloth and tucked it into his back pocket just in case. Then he had slipped out a window on the side of his house that was blocked from view of the street by a neighbor's side gate and rear privacy fence. He'd eased along the mature shrubs and trees, using them for cover until he was at Brenda's picket fence. Stepping over the short fence was simple enough, then he'd embedded himself in her landscape and waited.

He hadn't needed to wait long. Mallory showed up only fifteen or so minutes after his settling into position. She had driven into the alley, headlights off, and parked behind Brenda's garage. She and Janey had emerged from the car and gone to the back door. He had spotted no one else arriving.

He eased from his hiding place and started for the back door.

The nudge of something cold and hard against the back

of his skull stopped him. "I was wondering where you were. Hands up, Mr. PI."

He recognized the voice. *Ginger York.*

She patted him down thoroughly. She hummed a note of surprise. "First PI I ever met who doesn't carry a gun."

"I didn't notice your arrival," he said when she nudged him in the back with her weapon.

"That's because I was here hours before the two of you came back. Crouched between those damned hydrangeas. But I have to say, I wasn't expecting you to appear the way you did—emerging from those crepe myrtles." She nudged him again. "Now start walking. We're going inside through the back door."

He moved forward.

She made another of those surprised sounds. "Really, I can't believe I didn't hear you come out of your house and climb over the fence. You must be half cat."

"Just practice," he said. He glanced over his shoulder at the blonde. "It's the same with weapons."

She made a face. "What the hell does that mean?"

"If," he explained, then he abruptly ducked and swung around, slamming his right shoulder into her midsection. The weapon flew from her hand before she could squeeze the trigger. The impact of his body took her to the ground. One hand came down over her mouth, his legs on either side of her body, pinning her to the ground. He yanked the wash-cloth from his back pocket and stuffed it into her mouth.

She bit him and he winced.

"If," he repeated as he flipped her onto her stomach, "you know how to use your body you don't always need a weapon."

He unfastened his belt, slid it from the loops of his jeans and used it to secure her hands behind her back. He helped her to a standing position. His fingers coiled in her hair, he pushed her toward the street. Once he was at his car, he popped the trunk and pushed her inside. She kicked at him, but he managed to close the lid. Then she started kicking it. But getting out of there wouldn't be so easy.

He hurried back around the house. He picked up the weapon Ginger had fumbled and checked the magazine. In his earpiece the conversation between Mallory and Brenda was ongoing. Sounded as if Brenda had led her to the bathroom to retrieve the hidden list from beneath that fern. He needed one or the other to keep talking so he could get a feel for their location.

Moving silently, he entered the house.

BRENDA PICKED UP the fern and retrieved the plastic bag that contained the list Scott had made. She handed it to Mallory. "This is it."

"Open it up. I want to see."

She set the fern aside then, taking care not to damage the paper. Brenda tugged the folded half page from the bag and very carefully unfolded it. Since this had already been done once, it opened fairly easily. She passed the paper to Mallory.

The gun pointed at her made Brenda flinch each time she looked at it. She reached down and smoothed Janey's hair. She hoped her baby wouldn't get upset. So far she just wanted to hang on to her mommy's legs. No crying. No asking questions.

Just let us get through this.

A grin slid across Mallory's face. "I guess we have a deal." She used the gun to motion for Brenda to go out of the room. "Back to the kitchen," she ordered.

With Janey still attached to her leg, Brenda walked out

of the bathroom and along the hall toward the living room. All those framed photos of her baby made her heart ache. *Just let us survive this.*

Mallory, her gun aimed at Brenda's head, stayed right behind them.

As soon as Brenda and Janey rounded the corner into the kitchen they were shoved aside, and an explosion fractured the silence.

Brenda scrambled up against the island, Janey wrapped in her arms.

Ben had Mallory face down on the floor. There was a hole in the ceiling where her weapon had fired, and Mallory was shouting that she was going to kill him, but her gun was nowhere to be seen.

Brenda held tightly to Janey. Was it over?

5:30 a.m.

JANEY WAS ASLEEP. Finally.

Brenda really should tuck her into her bed, but she couldn't bear the idea of being even inches from her. Rather, she held her baby in her lap. She sat on the sofa, a throw wrapped around her child.

Exhaustion had started tugging harder at Brenda, but she could not go to sleep until this was done.

The front door opened, and Ben walked in. "They're taking them now."

He took Janey into his arms so Brenda could go onto the porch to watch the police haul Mallory and Ginger away.

As the first Huntsville PD cruiser pulled away from the curb, Mallory twisted around to stare at her from the back seat. Brenda stared back at her, hoped she never saw the light of day again. Then the second cruiser rolled away. But

Ginger didn't turn around and look. She stared forward. She was hoping for a deal by spilling her guts on her friend.

Detective Shelton came to the bottom of the steps. "I believe we're done here, Ms. Devers."

The FBI agent's sedan pulled away just then, following the parade of police cars.

Brenda drew in a deep breath. "I'm glad."

Shelton laughed. "I'm sure you are." He gave her a little salute before turning and walking away.

Brenda went back inside and closed the door. She locked it and then announced, "I think we can put Janey to bed now."

It was time to try to get their lives back in some sort of order. To put the past behind them and to move on.

Ben carried Janey to her room. Brenda drew back the covers and he tucked the sleeping child in.

Weak with relief, she wandered back to the living room. Ben trailed close behind her. She dropped onto the sofa. She was too tired to even consider having a conversation while standing. She couldn't even remember when she'd last slept.

"Once Shelton told Mallory that Ginger was spilling her guts to the FBI agent," he explained, "she confessed. She killed Cummings but she swears that Ginger killed Scott. The police will have to sort out the discrepancies."

"As long as Janey and I don't have to be involved," Brenda allowed, "I'll be happy."

"I don't see any reason your testimony would be needed. Those two are going to rat out each other well enough, I think."

Brenda felt fairly clear enough on all that had happened. Scott and Tate had made a mistake and gotten involved with the cartel. But what Scott didn't tell Tate was that he had already been skimming accounts. Once he realized he was in trouble, he went to the FBI and tried to blame the whole situation on Tate. Only the agent he spoke to was not an FBI agent, it was whoever Cummings turned out to be—ultimately a part of the cartel hierarchy. The FBI handler, Clinton Pratt, was actually an FBI agent. This one Tate had called in. Scott might have gotten away with his long-running bad deeds had he not decided to get greedy and steal funds from one of the cartel accounts. At least he'd suffered a moment of guilt and called the Colby Agency for Brenda and Janey.

Mallory had been put in place to keep an eye on Scott. Ginger had been having an affair with Tate, doing the same—watching Tate. Except Scott didn't die in the explosion the way he was supposed to. What Brenda saw at LAX was Ginger retrieving Scott, but not for the cartel—for the little plan she and Mallory had come up with. The two made sure the timing was just right for trying to unsettle Brenda—to make her lose trust in herself and in her husband's intentions for his family. The two weren't happy Scott had reached out to the Colby Agency. As for the cartel, they didn't care what Mallory and Ginger did as long as they got their money. The two faithful hirelings were welcome to the remaining spoils.

"We have every reason to believe the cartel has no desire to bother you and Janey," Ben explained. "To them, the rest was irrelevant. I think the only people who need to worry about the cartel are Mallory and Ginger if either of them chooses to bring up their employer. But they won't do that if they want to live."

Brenda wished she could drum up some sympathy for Mallory but that was not happening.

"So it's really over?"

Ben nodded. "We believe so."

An unexpected disappointment nudged her. She wasn't

ready for whatever was happening between them to be over. But Ben had been here doing a job. She, of all people, understood that situations like this could get personal. She wrote about it, after all. She could hardly expect him to still have those same feelings now that the nightmare was over.

"I guess you'll be leaving then." Just saying the words was like inviting an elephant to sit on her chest.

"Soon. Yes," he agreed.

There it was. He was going. Oh well. She didn't write romance novels, and perhaps this was why—sometimes there just weren't any happy endings to be found.

"I was wondering," Ben said, "if you and Janey might want to get away for a couple of weeks or months. Just until things settle down here and everything has worked itself out. Otherwise, there will be reporters hounding you. The stories in the papers and on social media will draw all the true crime fans right to your door. You might be more comfortable taking some time away."

She smiled. "You've given this a great deal of thought."

"I have." He searched her face, hope in his eyes.

"It's really a good idea." Having Janey back was all that had been on her mind until a few hours ago. "The trouble is I have no idea where we would go."

"I think I know just the place," he offered. "I have this great house in the suburbs of Chicago. There's a big yard. The former owners had children so there's a really cool outdoor playset."

Hope soared in her chest, and her smile came back wider than before. "Are you inviting us to your home?"

"Yes. If you and Janey would like, I would love for you to spend some time with me. I have way too much unused vacation time."

Brenda stood. "I don't know what to say."

Ben pushed to his feet and took a step in her direction. "Say whatever you feel."

Her lips trembled with the emotions whirling inside her now. "I feel like spending time with you. I feel like getting to know you better."

He took another step toward her. "Then just say yes."

"Yes."

The final step between them disappeared, and he took her face in his hands and kissed her. Tenderly, deeply.

Brenda couldn't wait to start her and Janey's new beginning.

* * * * *

Don't miss
The Bride's Betrayal,
the next thrilling story in USA TODAY
bestselling author Debra Webb's miniseries
Colby Agency: The Next Generation
Coming next month from Harlequin Intrigue
Available wherever Harlequin books and ebooks are sold.